Fire Bound

By

Karli Rush

For the girl who loves David. Charidy, may you sleep without any other intrusions from our witchy friend.

Come to the woods,

The spirit's calling you,

Come to the Ways,

that the ancients knew,

preserved for you,

Come to the Ways.

Come to the woods, the spirit's calling you,

Come to the woods,

Where the fay run free,

And the old Ones be,

Come to the woods.

Come to the woods,

The spirit's calling you.

Come to the Ways,

And tread moonlight paths

To circles dance,

Come to the woods...

~ Raven Grimassi

Chapter One

Destiny is what's meant to be, they say it's what's written in the stars, your inescapable fate. There's no avoiding destiny — it's going to happen no matter what you do. I thought I could change that. Change my destiny to fit what I wanted. But destiny had other plans for me and veered me down another road.

Roads eventually turned into highways and highways turned into different cities. Each one hiding darkness. A darkness most men would run from, but not me. Instead, I hunt for what lurks in the dark. Exposing evil witches for what they truly are— the *summoners of demons*. Meddling in the dark arts, black magick, and taking innocent lives as they see fit. The oath in our coven is to harm none and that's why I am hunting down these bastards one by one. I know what the dark Brotherhood of the Raven clan can do. I saw what their kind did to one of our own, and it almost destroyed her. They're a different breed of witches, obsessed with only greed and power. So now, we've formulated a clan called witch hunters, and the Brotherhood *will* fall.

"What are you talking about, Alyssa?" I hop off my custom-made, Bomb Runner bike and grab some stuff out of my bags. I juggle the phone while I unlock the door to the cabin. "Explosions are gonna happen. *No…* I didn't mean for the neighbor's house to catch on fire. Look, you of all people should know how our fire gets a little out of control?" I let out a sigh and sling my things over to the dusty couch. "Alyssa, look, just tell your Dad everything's taken care of. Just don't mention the other stuff, okay?"

I stroll toward the kitchen and start rummaging through the fridge. "Yeah, well, tell everyone I'm still alive and kickin' ass." I laugh and press end on my cell phone. The bottled water in my hand almost comes to a boil as I take the cap off. I'm still hotter than hell. Ghostly flames trail up and down my fingertips and I try to reign it in. I didn't expect to be ambushed by a hoard of fire-breathing witches. A guy can only take so much, so I gave them a dose of their own fire. I had no intention of obliterating someone's house, though. The end result—they're gone.

I drag out maps and papers plotting my next move. Every word is encrypted. Every direction is twisted in spells only the Worthington coven knows. I flick the pages back without touching them and get a feeling I'm coming to a dead-end soon. It's the same feeling when I found out Alyssa and I couldn't be bound. I knew it before she moved to Montana and I broke off our relationship. An impulsive response and I regretted it the moment I did it. She knew our connection wasn't a lifemate bond, but nevertheless, I believed I could still have her.

Two witches, lifemates forming an intimate bond like this only makes them stronger together. Bound by blood, their souls would never sever. It's the foundation of our kind. I had fallen so in love with her— *nothing* would get in my way. No mortal. No witch. And I thought it would happen for us until, that is, Marcus Del Dante came into the picture. Her true lifemate, and even then, I still thought she belonged to me. It's taken me years to finally accept my destiny and let go of the notion we belonged together. Which is why I am here miles and miles away. Instead of hunting for her love, I'm hunting down the ones that almost destroyed her.

I glance down at my phone, a picture of Alyssa and her son, Aden, flash across my screen. She's probably checking in again. I know the Worthington coven worries about a lone witch out and about, chasing down the most dangerous coven. But I've made it this far, maybe scorched a little here and there, but nothing I can't handle. I pick off the singed pieces from my shirt and hit ignore on the call. Still to this day I'm affected by the sound of her voice. Yeah, I may put on a good front and act all cocky, but I can't let myself slip. I have to stay focused, and more importantly, keep my heart guarded.

Locked, bolted, and impenetrable.

My neck starts to ache like a mother, and I decide it's time to shower. I slide one small map out and mark off the locations I plan to hit next. Shifting to the bedroom I start to grab some towels when I hear a knock on the door. No one knows I'm here. I picked this spot because of its isolation, a lone cabin in the woods. Not a soul could find this place, but apparently, someone has. I tilt my head side to side and whisper, *"Flames on."*

I reach the front door and open it with an age-old spell. "Patefio." I'm ready to light up whoever followed me here.

"David?"

"Evan?"

"What the hell?" I growl, my flames die out and I pierce him with an exasperated look. "Did you bring the cavalry here too?" I peer out the door checking to see if anyone else came with him. He's already shifted inside.

"No," he says behind me.

"Mr. Worthington?"

"No."

"Marc?"

"No."

"Megan?"

"No," he says calmly striding toward a chair and takes a seat making himself at home. "You know, you might want to conceal your trail more, David—"

"Conceal? What do you mean? No one followed me here except, *you*," I retort and cross my arms over my chest.

"Well, I wouldn't have followed you if it weren't for the smoke signals every five miles or so." He slides his black, leather gloves off and stares at me as if I'm losing my touch.

"Smoke? What smoke?" I brush off his absurd comments and take a seat across from him.

"The police think there's an arsonist in the area."

"Well, good. That'll keep'em off my trail."

Evan shakes his head. "A trail of smoke led me directly here, David?" He scoots back in his seat and adds, "I'm surprised there's still rubber on your bike out there."

"Don't you worry about my bike, Evan. I got everything under control." I stand and start walking toward the door. "Hey, you want something to drink. Maybe some tea?" Evan carefully watches me as I drum my fingers along the doorframe. "I'm sure there's a box of Lipton or whatever it is you drink down the road. Ah… Damn it. I can't think of that name of the store at the moment, but you'll figure it out once you get there."

"No, David. I'm not needing a drink and I'm not leaving…yet."

I glare up at the ceiling and lean against the wall. "What gives? Did Daniel put you up to this?"

"Not exactly, we have a few more leads."

"Leads on more of the Brotherhood? Can't be possible, Evan. I've pretty much, single-handedly, mind you, extinguished most of those sleazebags out," I explain. Evan slips out an envelope, and as his dark trench coat fans out more, and I can see clear vials stashed in the other pocket. I nod his way. "What are you now? CIA? Worthington's top-notched detective?"

I chuckle smugly. "Because the way you're dressed doesn't fit you, Evan. It's way overkill."

"Have you not heard a word I said?" He glances up at me. "Every area you've been to, the cops are in hot pursuit for an arsonist riding a motorcycle. It won't take long before someone remembers something." He redirects his gaze from me and pulls out an array of photos and documents. Carefully, he places each across the coffee table in front of us. "Now, do you recognize these?"

I walk over and study the images. "Yeah. I do. The book that summoned Jinn, but I thought…"

"They no longer exist? Well, we think someone has conjured a new one," Evan states and hands me a photo of a group of men and women gathered around a plain, old building. At the bottom, the words *Willowshire coven* are written. Nothing seems out of the ordinary to me, so I hand it back to him. "Okay? So, there's a new book of shadows to summon our good ol' buddy, Jinn?"

Evan clears his throat and leans forward. "No, not Jinn. A different demon."

Chapter Two

I drop to the chair closest to me. It hits me like a two-ton weight. The Brotherhood has another book. Why? I know why, greed. But the real question for me is how? I cast a glance over Evan's notes and start noticing strange symbols jotted down on each page.

"They're demon sigils. So far, every pentagram I've come across has the same sigils," Evan explains. He places the pages side by side and shows how each resembles the other. "They're not like Jinn's or any sigils I've ever seen before."

I rub the side of my jaw and ask, "The photo of the Willowshire coven, are you thinking someone from there knows something?"

"I was thinking someone knows or possibly even helped create this book. Which is why I haven't said anything to Daniel or anyone in the Worthington coven. I have to find out who's behind it before I tell the others."

"You mean *we*," I state motioning between us. "We have to find out before we bring it to the head honcho." I glance back down at the old photo, trying to remember what road would be quicker *too*—

"David… David, look, the only reason I came down this way was because of the trail you're leaving. We can't let them know we're snooping around, and I can't—"

"And you can't do this alone, yeah, yeah, I got it. You need my help. Don't worry I have your back, Evan." Evan raises a brow and shakes his head at me like he's stunned that I'd join up with him so easily. There's no way I would let someone like Evan go at it alone. I mean, the guy has guts to come all the way down here, but no one can handle a demon conjuring witch alone. He may have a good eye at spotting one of them out because he was knee-deep in the Brotherhood at one point. But that's another story.

I ease back and ask, "So, what's the plan?" Evan narrows his eyes at me and starts picking up everything, minus the maps, from the small coffee table. "You have a plan, right?"

"I do," he answers calmly.

"Care to elaborate? I mean, since this is going to be a team effort I think we should have the same line of attack... *unless—*"

"David, we can't go in with all guns blazing or in your case, burning everything up. This has to be done," he says adamantly tapping the table between us. "with caution, and I, *we,* cannot let this book slip out of our hands. Once we figure out where it's located we'll..."

"We'll destroy it, piece of cake, nothing to it." Evan practically slouches back in his chair defeated, but I ignore him and start studying the maps. I know what he's thinking, he wants to handle this coven, this situation like it's some kind of detective novel. But that's not going to happen, there's no time to dillydally, not when so much is at stake. If he's right, then there's going to be human lives in danger. "All right, if Willowshire is around the Redwood forest and we're in Salem, Oregon." I drag my finger down the map, figuring up the distance I finally say, "It's going to take us about four to five hours to get there." I begin setting up the GPS coordinates on my phone when Evan gets a call. He shifts in a blink outside. I get up from my chair and pace, his voice is so low that I can't make out what's being said. After a few minutes pass, I give up trying to get an earshot of who's on the line and restock my things. My bags are about to combust with crap, things other than the norm. Most guys would have clothes, food, et cetera, but I'm preparing for something entirely different… extermination. Cramming in the last book, I hear Evan walking back inside.

"Ah… David, you really think reading a book on *How to Dominate a Succubus* will help here?"

I snatch the book away from him and shrug. "It might, you never know."

Evan chuckles and slips his leather gloves back on. "You know, there's a Beltane celebration coming up."

"Yeah, well, I don't think we're going to be celebrating anything until we get this job done."

Evan spins a set of shiny, new keys around his fingertip. "That, my friend, is where I believe you're wrong." A smile creeps across his clean-shaven face as he adds, "It's time you indulge in some bonfire fun because we're not just going to any Beltane celebration. We're going to the Willowshire's celebration. C'mon."

I send him a quizzical look and follow him outside. Parked in the driveway is a fully restored 1967 Chevy Impala. It has a flawless midnight blue paint job with black leather interior. It reminds me of one of those classic hotrods from some muscle car magazine. I do a walk around and check out the motor, the inside, and the trunk. Scratching my head, I taunt, "You definitely have the room for a few bodies in there, is that the plan?"

"Yeah, David. I'm going to pile all the bodies from the Brotherhood in my car, that's the plan," he retorts back and slides into the driver's seat. I'm half expecting a deep rumbling sound to surge through the night air from his car, but surprisingly it hums quietly. "Are you waiting for a full moon or somethin'?" he questions.

"What? No, I'm just shocked you're driving something so relic. I mean, you sure it's going to get you to Redwood?"

"It got me here, didn't it? Besides, I've been using parts off your old Chevelle," he quips and quickly backs out of the driveway.

I half-heartedly laugh and stride toward my bike. He better not have used any parts off my car. I drop his joking aside and think about the Beltane. My family, the Van Buren clan, wasn't much into the ancient traditions. The most we did were marriages and handfasting and I guess it's why I felt so driven in finding my lifemate. It was known by my parents if you were crescent bound you were held in an entirely different light. Seen like a noble, almost. I get how our kind strives for it, how it drives some of us mad seeking it out. Who doesn't want to have that connection with someone? The bond which only makes you and your element stronger, but on the other hand, I've had a front-row show of how Marc was losing control over his element when he lost Alyssa. It wasn't pretty, and I can honestly say, if the role were reversed, I would have been a constant walking inferno.

I let out a sigh and start up my bike, preparing myself for whatever comes next. Witches, demons, or even a succubus— I think I can handle whatever the Gods have in store for me.

Chapter Three

Arriving, I notice two things. The small-town deviates from the norm, there are shops up and down the streets like a cuisine of witchcraft. Walkways made out of dark cobblestone which leads down to the lower part of town. Signs hang above— Palm Reader to Psychic Readings and everything in between. Cafés and quaint restaurants advertising herbal drinks and whatnot. The other thing I notice is how no one treats us like we're strangers. Everyone here has a happy-go-lucky smile or a cheery *hello* while we make our way toward the hotel. I don't pick up any vibe there are witches among us, no instinctive pull or uncanny feeling. But I know the Brotherhood and if/when they're having a sip or two of their fancy, little drink tainted with demon's blood, they become invisible to us.

"You wanna check us in while I scope out our new turf?" I bump Evan with my elbow and nod toward a coffee shop. Evan glances over to me, and I know the look he's giving me. It's tentative and leery. "What could possibly happen while I'm having a cup of coffee?" Evan doesn't relax his stance, instead, he narrows his gaze at me even more. "Hey, c'mon, now. We made it here without anything catching fire, didn't we?"

"Surprisingly," he mouths and strides inside the hotel. The hotel itself doesn't carry a modernistic feel in any sense. It's nestled between two main streets making it look like an oddly shaped centerpiece. My guess is it's probably one of the oldest buildings around here. I redirect my gaze to the coffee shop. The Witchery, coffee shop *and more*.

Well, this should be interesting.

I spot an empty table and take a seat. Everything down to the tables have indications of something witch-like. The table I'm sitting at has letters and numbers imprinted on it like a Ouija board. Black and white candles illuminate each area and I'm starting to think they're hardcore fans of witches, or someone didn't tell them Halloween is over. I lean back a bit and take the scene in. Besides the two little old women, I'm the only visitor until I see Evan stroll up.

"Hey, you order anything yet?" he questions sitting across from me.

"No, I was just getting ready to contact a spirit, but I can't seem to find the piece of wood to move around."

"Planchette?" he remarks raising a brow.

"Yeah, is that what they call it?"

He looks at me unimpressed for a second, and then we're both suddenly drawn out of our banter. A waitress stands just a few feet from our table. She's tall, blonde, and captivating. Her eyes stare at Evan first, then over to me. Is she nervous? I watch as she parts her full, beautiful lips a time or two before she actually says something to us.

"Ahem, Welcome to The Witchery. What can I get you two?"

I look at Even and wonder is he seeing what I'm seeing? Because the Gods have Aphrodite workin' in the wrong place. There's no earthly way someone as stunning as her would be in a joint like this. Evan nods his head toward our lovely waitress and subtly reminds me I need to answer her.

"Yeah, I'll have…" I pretend I'm looking past her shoulder and at the counter upfront. While I'm reading the never-ending list of coffees available, I move my gaze to her. I can't keep my eyes off of her.

Evan cuts in and responds before I get a chance, "I'll have the Americano. David, want me to order for you?"

I scowl at him and finally reply, "I'll have the same." Immediately I regret what comes out of my mouth. *I'll have the same?* I'm so thrown off with her I can't even think straight.

She places a couple of napkins on the table and offers an out-of-this-world kind of smile. A smile that could knock a man to his knees. Good thing I'm sitting down. I get a whiff of her sweet perfume and it makes me want to lean in closer, closer *to her* and drag in the most seductive scent I've ever had the pleasure to smell.

"My name is Hannah and if there's anything else I can get for you, just say the word. I'll be right back with your orders," she says still carrying that remarkable smile. If I stood up, she would be about my height. She looks young but maybe it's the way the early morning light shines on her face. Not a lot of make-up, she's more natural with full, pink lips, light-colored eyes, and long, silky blonde hair. She spins around and saunters away. I tear my gaze from her and crane my head toward Evan.

"Easy ten," Evan spouts.

"Ten? What are you blind? I'd say she's off the charts," I retort back, mumbling under my breath. *Easy ten? What the fuck?*

Evan coughs in his hand and leans his elbows on the table. His voice lowers. "Are you getting any vibes she's a witch?"

"No, you?"

He glances toward the counter as if he's studying some kind of homicide scene. His eyes narrow more while he rubs his chin. Eventually, he switches his direction toward me. "No. she's human."

"Wonderful, Sherlock, glad we cleared that up." I drum my fingers along the tabletop and note a few more people entering the shop. Two women, one tall and lanky, the other short and plump. Both are middle-aged with a flare of tacky jewelry and bold, red lips. They amble around the counter for a moment or two and then occupy a table beside us. The tall one, wearing a slew of pearl necklaces gestures a small, friendly wave. I casually nod trying not to draw any unwanted attention. I take a moment to investigate the rest of the place, but before I have the chance to analyze more, Hannah promptly delivers our coffees to us.

"Here you go," she announces. She gently rubs her hands along her apron and adds, "Would you like a croissant, they're freshly made?"

I'm too busy checking out every perfect curve of her to answer. Evan once again beats me to the punch. "No, I think this will do. Right, David?"

"Huh? What?" I mutter moronically. *What is she doing to me?* "Yeah, yeah, this is great. Thanks."

"So, are you two tourists, just passing through?" she asks.

Evan and I both glance at one another briefly. I finally get my shit together and answer before he does, "You could say that." Thank the Gods I sound confident and hopefully, convincing.

"Well, we're glad you're here. If you're interested in some of the festivities that are coming up…" She takes a delicate finger and points up toward a board filled with flyers and posters. "They'll be on that. We try to keep newcomers informed of the events here."

"Are you going to be at one of these events?" I ask with all humor aside and offer her my best smile.

She sends me a striking smile back. "It's possible. I usually attend one if I'm not working."

"Well, maybe we could pick you up for one of these festivities and you could show us around?"

She actually chuckles at me like I'm a ten-year-old kid who has a crush on his school teacher. *What the…?* "Oh, I couldn't. Work has been non-stop lately. Besides, I wouldn't want to intrude."

I peer over to Evan, mentally telling him, *come on, man, help a brother out here.* He's like a lump of dead weight— uncooperative and difficult. So, I trudge onward. "Intrude? You would not be intruding in any way, I swear."

"Oh, aren't you two together?" she questions, innocently glancing between us.

Evan just about spits his coffee all over the table, while I try to get a grip on what she just asked. Why in the world would she think that? "*Uh…* yeah, we're here together but—"

She shrugs her shoulders lightly and comments before I can say another word, "It's okay. Really. Everyone here at Mistcove accepts all types of relationships." Without missing a beat, she slides our bill down, then spins around on her heels and dashes off. Suddenly, I feel a caress along my hand, and I drag my eyes over to Evan. His fingers dance along my knuckles as he sends a wink my way. I jerk my hand back as fast as I can.

"Stop it," I growl. "Do you realize you just blew away my chance?"

Evan nonchalantly peeks at the bill in his hand and grins. "Chance at what? Getting laid?"

"Yeah, getting laid. What are you now, celibate?"

Evan leisurely removes money from his wallet and cocks his head to the side. "We're not here to get laid, David."

"Maybe you're not. Besides, didn't you say I needed to relax a bit?"

He leans on the table and spouts, "When you're burning things down left and right, then yeah, I'd say relax. Chill out, but we can't get sidetracked by every woman that entices us."

"Hey, man, if you can't see the chemistry burning between Hannah and me then you've completely lost it. I mean, didn't you see the way she was lookin' at me?"

"Like you're swinging the other way?" Evan tosses a tip on the table and moseys himself out of the coffee shop, but just as he reaches for the door, he turns and waves a hand my way. And I don't mean in a manly way either. He's full-blown dancing in the daisies, all perky and merry. Then to top it off, he shouts, "Coming, honey?"

I'm going to kill him and stuff his body in that gigantic, worthless car of his. I make my way to the door. I pass by Hannah and give her a real mannish nod. Making sure I sound all cool and masculine and say. "He's just kidding. Don't pay any attention to him."

She looks confused for a split second, but then replies softly, "Oh, all right."

"Maybe sometime we could meet up and you can tell me more about this town?"

"I'm sorry, I don't go out with customers."

She walks with me to the entrance and I step a foot outside and state, "Okay, I'm not a customer anymore, wanna go have a bite to eat somewhere?"

She laughs and I watch mesmerized as she threads her fingers through her golden locks of hair. "I…" she pauses as if she's stumped on what to say next, but then gathers her composure and continues, "I don't go out with strangers, sorry."

I hold my hand out, waiting, hoping she'll take it. When she slips her hand inside mine I feel an intense current of excitement run through me. Honestly, I'm not used to women acting so indifferent with me, usually, they're wide open for any invitation I offer.

"I'm David Van Buren."

"Hannah Wolfenstein, nice to meet you, David," she announces.

"So, we're not strangers anymore, Hannah. When can I pick you up?"

She laughs again and aims a finger inside the coffee shop. "I really need to get back to work."

"Wolfenstein, huh? I bet there's a story behind that name," I pry trying to see if I can get a few more moments with her. But to no avail, she starts heading inside.

"Maybe, if you're lucky. I'll see you around, David Van Buren," she states softly and disappears from my sight.

Chapter Four

"So, what's got you so interested to search the web all night, David?" I scratch below my chin and scan the screen in front of me. My hand grips an empty coffee cup sitting beside the laptop. I glance down at it like a weary-eyed zombie starving to death.

"What?" I grumble.

"It's seven in the morning, David. Are you done taking virtual tours of this quaint little town yet?"

Since I've been on this witch hunt I haven't slept much, and it's starting to catch up with me. Funny how our kind can shoot fire from ours hands, shift to different places unnoticed, and mouth a few words that can make someone forget things entirely, but we can't deprive ourselves too long of sleep. I rub my eyes and ease back in my chair. "For your information, Evan. I'm not trolling the internet on this town. I'm looking this up." I aim a finger at the screen.

A list of Wolfenstein legends flood the page, dating back as far as the fifteenth century. Evan leans over me, studying the images that appear. "Okay, so what does this have to do with the book?"

"The girl from the coffee shop."

Evan takes my cup and strides toward the bathroom area with it and asks, "You're thinking she's part of this?" The sound of the coffeemaker kicks on and I sit up more, it's going to take a lot more than caffeine to keep me awake.

"Her last name is Wolfenstein and yeah, maybe," I grumble.

He peeks around the corner and reminds me, "She's human, we both decided that when we first saw her." He finally strolls back in carrying two steaming cups and I quickly notice the smug look before he says a word.

"What?"

"I know what you're doing." He sits my cup down and grabs a chair. "You're trying to find any excuse to drag her into this mess. I mean look, David." He points at the screen and shakes his head like he's skeptical. "Wolfenstein? I've never heard of them. Have you? Have you ever heard the Worthington's mention the name before? I already know the answer, you haven't because if you did, you wouldn't be here scouring the web all night."

I wave him off. "Just because the Worthington's haven't mentioned the name doesn't mean anything, Evan. Besides, I think it's worth looking into and if you're just going to be a jealous killjoy then leave the research to me."

He laughs, "Jealous? Of what?"

I shrug. "You know, of Hannah and I, what we have together. I know it's tough on you but—"

Evan stands, pats my back, and replies, "Get some sleep, David."

I mumble some choice words under my breath. My eyes burn, I rub them and try to read the last section of the Wolfenstein legends. *Witch trials… werewolves…lycanthropy… and phases of the moon…*

———

"David, wake up."

I breathe in, it sounds rough and distant. Slowly, I open my eyes and glance across the keyboard. My head still spins with images of werewolves and folklore. I take in another deep breath and grumble. "You won't believe the dream I had."

Evan grips my shoulder and leans over me. "I can imagine. Who wouldn't, reading this stuff? I'm surprised you haven't come across vampires and zombies."

"Ha," I retort rubbing the sleep from my eyes.

Evan turns the computer screen off and tosses me my leather jacket. "Daylight's a burnin'. You've slept a good ten hours. Think you're ready to inspect this town a little more?"

"Yeah. Wait…" I start to ask sliding my jacket on. "What have you been doing while I was sacked out?"

"Well, they have a great lunch special on Spring street." He halts his next step and says, "Did you know that most of the streets here were originally animal trails that progressed into roads?"

"No, Ev. I had no idea."

"And I heard there are witches here."

"Shocking," I mockingly reply.

"Might be best if we tread lightly," he explains easing his dark sunglasses on. A brow peeks over the rim of the shades as he adds, "We can't jeopardize our mission bewitched by a werewolf."

I shove by him unamused. "Shut the fuck up." The door closes behind me leaving only the sound of my footsteps in the hall. A few minutes later I hear Evan approaching. He sidesteps around an elderly woman and meets me in the elevator. He carries a smirk I know all too well.

"Are you done?" I ask.

"Are you?"

I tilt my head in his direction, my tone gruff as I calmly reply, "I'm tryin' to find the book."

"So am I, but I'm not letting anything distract me, David."

"I'm not letting anything distract me either. I'm just following up on some leads which is way more promising. Besides this town is as dry as fucking dust."

A noise inside the elevator startles us. Slowly, we turn around and notice the little old woman Evan passed by earlier. She covers her mouth, clearing her throat before she says, "You two sound like a bunch of old fuddy-duddies." The elevator comes to a halt, the door opens, and she shuffles out, but before the door starts to close, she adds in the sweetest tone, "You're more than welcome to come to the Beltane festival tomorrow night, that is if you two can stop squabbling amongst yourselves." Her grey eyes soften as a wrinkly smile appears and then she ambles slowly away. A floral purse sways back and forth in time with each step and I'm knocked for a loop. *How? When?* Why didn't Evan and I get the hint there was a witch standing right behind us?

Evan and I both stare at each other. Finally, he shrugs. "I told you there were witches here."

Chapter Five

"All right, so we know we're not alone and I guess we've been formally invited by the town's firstborn."

"She wasn't that old, David."

"Okay, well, either way, we have some detective work to do, right, Ev?" I nudge him as we leave the hotel. My boot hits the next cement step, I eye the coffee shop and begin my stride in that direction. A tight hand grips my arm, and before I know it I'm facing the other way.

"You take this side of town and I'll take the other," Evan states placidly.

"Oh, yeah?" I retort, knowing full well what he's up to. "You're going to check and see if Hannah is working today, huh?"

Evan shakes his head and glances at me. "Hannah is the least of our worries, David. Let's meet back here before dark. I don't want to have to come save you from a werewolf, *or worse, that old woman.*"

"You're just a million laughs today." I take a few steps back and turn around. "It's a good thing you're such a *fuddy-duddy* or we'd be havin' some fun." I shrug my shoulders like it's all on him and begin my path down a winding road. The town is tightly packed with shops, some are two-stories tall and filled with a dark mystery around every corner. People pass by carrying different types of shopping bags. Laughter and smiles drift through the air as if it's contagious. A couple holding hands nearly bump into me, the guy just grins like he's a love-struck fool and leads the girl he's with away. Reminds me of Marc and Alyssa, how they seemed so invulnerable to the world around them.

I shake off the memories and maneuver around the bustling crowds. An undeniable scent of homemade fudge and other delicious edibles rise throughout. My pace quickens as my hunger suddenly strikes me like I haven't eaten in days. This peculiar place grows more tempting by the second, but by the time I reach the next block I notice something. An alleyway. It's concealed in darkness, just a shimmer of light emits from the metal lanterns above. Each step becomes steeper and more hidden. I take a moment and glance behind me wondering if this path is private for a reason, because that's what it feels like. No one as far as I can tell travels this way, it's so dark I have to snap my fingers to conjure my flames and see where the next step leads.

At the bottom is a brick wall, but to the left of me is a door— a large wooden door. I take a brief look making sure it's safe to enter and then I step inside. Two white wall lanterns hang on either side of the room. The thing that catches me off guard is that they're suspended by resin wolf heads holding the lanterns in the grips of their snarling teeth. As I walk farther into the dimly lit room I realize I'm in a bookstore. Various sized books, worn and tattered, line each wooden shelf. "*Bingo*," I whisper to myself, maybe something in here will lead me to the demon book. The odds are slim, but I'm not going to rule it out. So, I start to prowl around checking books. I slide a couple out and flip through a few pages. I'm not finding anything useful, so I stroll on over to the next aisle. I look up immediately when I hear someone come inside.

I'm sure if I'm not welcome here someone will bring it to my attention. I crouch down to the lower shelf and ease a book out. Standing up I spot two eyes watching in-between a void of books. "*Hello…*" a seductive voice purrs.

I rub my chin and answer intrigued, "Are you the curator of this place?"

"Perhaps," the silky-like voice replies.

I want her to feel comfortable with me, so I introduce myself, "I'm David, just a tourist, so don't mind *me—*"

"You're no tourist," the voice draws out and then another voice speaks from directly behind me.

"We're no curators just like you're no tourist. But you're in luck today, maybe my sister and I can help you." I turn around and discover a tall woman leaning against the opposite bookshelf. She's definitely easy on the eyes.

"You're gorgeous," I announce boldly.

"You hear that Chloe? He thinks I'm gorgeous," she announces proudly. The other woman steps out and she's just as beautiful. She checks me out like I'm the dish of the day or an hors d'oeuvre. I can't really tell with the way she's acting. She saunters slowly by, making a *hmmm* sound and then smiles.

"Yeah, Jess, I heard."

I lick my lips and glance between the two. "So, sisters, huh?"

Both nod in unison, still donning smiles that make me get the sense they'd like to rip my clothes off.

Chloe twirls a strand of golden hair around a finger and asks, "You don't come off as a book nerd, to me, David. Tell me why a man like you would want to be in a place like this?"

"I could ask the same about you," I retort, placing the books down on the shelf.

Jess steps closer, she rubs her fingers along my jacket and purrs in that same sultry tone as before, "*Mmm*, leather. I like it. C'mon, we'll show you why we're here and then we'll show you something better than this rustic place."

Both girls slide their arms around mine and direct me toward the back. The bookshelves become fewer, the lighting becomes brighter and I can actually see an area open for chairs. In the far corner is an oval-shaped chair, wine colored and soft. A woman sits in it with her legs curled beneath her, her shoes are discarded and thrown off to bone side. She flicks through the pages quietly as she reads the book in her lap, and as we approach more I note her perfume. I recognize the perfect angle of her face and the way the light shimmers off her skin.

"Hannah? Aunt Gemma wants to know if you're okay with watching the place for a bit longer?" Jess inquires and then stares at Chloe. "I don't know why we have to come down here and ask, she'll sit here all day just reading."

Chloe looks up to me and says in a pitying tone, "Hannah is our other sister, but she's nothing like us. See, watch…"

"Hannah? Look what we found… isn't he just to die for?" Chloe prompts, but Hannah doesn't budge, not a glance, not even a blink. Slowly she turns a page as she nibbles on her lower lip deep in thought. She looks so delicately graceful and beyond any beauty I can compare to.

"C'mon, Hannah. You have to say something, at least look at what we found," Jess urges waving a hand over me like I'm some kind of grand prize. "I can't believe you actually sat back here, reading that silly old book and didn't notice this hunk just a few feet from you."

Hannah turns another page and mumbles softly, "*Uh huh. Okay.*" She doesn't look up, not even when she steals a sip from her tea sitting beside her.

Chloe pats my arm. "You'll have to excuse my sister," she announces and then points a finger toward Hannah. "She's a book nerd, obviously, and you're not. So, let's get you out of here and have some fun, shall we?"

I clear my throat and state, "I've met Hannah before, down at the coffee shop."

Both girls raise an inquisitive brow and mouth, "Ooh!"

"I bet Hannah impressed your socks off, didn't she?" Jess teases and Chloe laughs. As for Hannah, she doesn't seem a bit offended by their taunts. The sound of her flipping another page resonates through the shadowy store.

Chloe threads her arm through mine again, and offers in a light-hearted tone, "See? She's completely oblivious to anything around her."

Jess tugs my hand, trying to pull me away. "C'mon let's do something fun!"

"I bet you have a lot of questions about our little Mistcove. I mean after all, you did find this hidden treasure," Chloe spouts with a jeering tone.

"It's not often we meet a man with so much power radiating from them. What's your gift? Water, *air*—?" Jess starts inquiring but before I can respond Chloe cuts her off.

"How long are you stayin'? What coven are you from? Do you—," Chloe rambles on and on until I stop them both. I raise my hands up halting their inquiries.

"Ladies, hold up," I announce with a stern tone. "I'll go wherever you want to take me, *and* I'll answer your questions, just as long as she comes, too." I aim directly at Hannah, making sure I lock my eyes on her. I want her to know I'm not leaving here without her. If this is my only shot to get to know her more, then I'm going to take it.

"Seriously?!" Chloe and Jess both shout. Hannah closes her book and shoots me the most miserable glare.

She drops the book on the small table next to her and huffs out a sigh, "Look, David, I appreciate the invite, but I can't just leave, someone has to watch the store." I watch her intently as she eases from the chair and reaches for the book. I move my hand outward and push the book away, she reaches for it again, but this time I use my power, calling the book to me. I give her one of my cocky grins when she scowls at me.

Jess and Chloe both *ooh* and *ahh* at my ability to move something without the call of a spell. Chloe grips my arm tighter and purrs, "*Okay*, I have to know more. Let's just leave Hannah to her books and tea."

I shake my head. "Nope." I tempt her with the book in my hands. "You want this? I'll give it to you if you'll join us, Hannah."

She crosses her arms over her chest. "And Mr. Showoff, who's going to watch the store?"

"Leave that to me," I remark and motion for her to follow us out.

Grudgingly she walks by carrying a scathing look. The second we step outside the door I peer over to Jess and Chloe. "Can you give me a little room to work here?" They both offer a lustful smile and release my arms. I hand Hannah her book back and face the wooden entryway and whisper a spell, "Ego mandatum signati." I place my hand on the door and summon the fire within me and mark an imprint. It's not visible to humans. It's a little added incantation and will keep anyone from entering. I brush my hands off and turn with a smile. "So, where to, ladies?"

Hannah looks the least impressed as she studies the door. "What if Aunt Gemma comes back?"

Chloe snags Hannah's wrist and incites in a mocking tone, "What if? *What if,* Hannah. Stop worrying! C'mon!" Chloe rushes past us, taking the lead. Hannah squeezes between Jess and me without a scowl this time. I quietly thank the goddesses, hoping she's going to give me a chance. In any case, were heading somewhere together, and that's a start.

Chapter Six

All three girls are about the same in height with similar long, light-colored hair but their eyes are what sets them apart. Chloe's are sky-blue, Jess' are tainted with flecks of green, Hannah's are blue-grey, her eyes are not what attracted me to her at first. It was the way she looked at me with shrewdness and tact. And her sisters are right, she is nothing like them. She hides who she is extremely well. She had Evan and I both believing she was human.

Chloe and Hannah keep a steady pace ahead while Jess clings to my right arm. Every once in a while she peeks at me all gushing and grins. "Well…I guess your hardwired element is fire. Sweet!"

She glides her hands along my jacket and steals a sniff. "Mmm… I can't believe I had no clue. Usually, I'm rather good at telling a witch's element. Wanna guess mine?"

"Your what?" I mumble, keeping my sight locked forward. She catches my chin and slowly positions it so that I'm looking directly at her.

"My element?"

"Yeah, sure," I grumble. We stroll through the streets until we reach a dead-end. A limestone fountain sits off to one side hidden by vines and ferns. Just beyond the fountain, there's a metal gate, which I would've never found since it's covered in foliage. It squeaks open like it hasn't been used in a hundred years and I quickly follow them, but I have to bend down to miss all the endless tendrils of green. It's like walking into the elysian fields, but they apparently laid off their gardener, or he just said *fuck it* and quit— not sure which. I brush some thorn-covered twigs away and note Hannah peering over her shoulder. She watches me just as intensely as I watch her and then Jess tugs me in a different direction.

"Hey!" I shout toward Jess, but she's got a death-grip on my hand and won't let go.

"It's quicker this way. C'mon, follow me!" she yells back, picking up her pace. The next thing I know we're running through a forest of darkness till a splash of light emerges. We reach a cliff overlooking the town below, she pauses just enough to catch a breath, then she laughs and steers us down a sharp incline. It's so steep my boots slip sideways desperately trying to get a grip. She releases my hand and clings to a thick vine, but once it narrows, she grips both hands on it and a sprout of roots begin to grow. A gnarly, tough rope of roots become her leverage, and she uses her element to help us glide down to the bottom.

She kicks off her sandals and shakes the dirt from her earth-tone dress. "We beat them!" I brush off my jeans and send her a sideways smile.

"Yeah, I guess we did."

"Now you know…" she states smugly.

"Know what?"

"My element," she replies and saunters toward a massive rock. It sits dead center, flat like a stage. She hops up on it and reaches out to me, "I know your element, and you know mine. What else can I show you, David?"

I jump up and meet her on the rock. The instant I do, she's all hands, trying to push my jacket off and running her fingers along my shirt. "What about Hannah?" I ask as she continues exploring.

"What about Hannah?"

"Her element?" I pry, taking a step back.

She lets out a heavy sigh and answers, "She's the same, earth. Now…I want to try something."

I scrunch my brows and peer at her. "*Okay*," I say with a leery tone. She tucks a golden lock behind her ear and begins casually unbuttoning the top of her dress.

A coy look possesses her face as she says, "Touch me."

"Where?" I ask, unsure where this is going. Gently I touch her arm and study her expression, waiting for her to explain.

"Now, make me vibrate with your hands, David," she whispers and then places both of her hands on my chest. "Call your fire, *I—*" She steals a nervous breath before she continues, "I heard that fire elements can make you feel this incredible sensation when they're endowed with their element." My mouth hangs open, but nothing comes out. Silence sweeps between us awkwardly and I search her face for more clarification. "Here, maybe this will help," she offers.

Each button slips from the loose fabric, her eyes are glued to mine as if she's waiting for me to combust into flames. She removes a few more buttons as if I need to jumpstart my fire, but we're suddenly interrupted when Chloe and Hannah approach. "Well? Did it work, Jess? Did his flames give you the ecstasy you thought it would?" Chloe questions with genuine interest.

Jess props her hands on her hips and replies, "We haven't got that far, Chloe."

"So, you don't know if it works?" Chloe mouths as she climbs up the rock. I watch as Hannah perches herself beside a tree, she seems aloof and bored out of her mind. She gathers her long hair and tucks it over a shoulder and begins opening the book she brought with her.

Before she gets too comfortable I call out to her, "What is this place?"

Her hands grip the book like it's an anchor as if she's desperately trying to push the outside world away. She's trying to ignore me. Chloe and Jess giggle and whisper to each other and then one of them shouts, "Are you going to tell him, or should we, Hannah?"

Slowly she drags her eyes away from the pages that beckon her. A sigh escapes from her lips before she answers, "It's where we hold the Beltane celebration."

Chloe leaps down from the rock and spins around. Her white dress fans outward as she spreads her arms like she's dancing on air. "It's magical, don't you think?" she asks in an enraptured tone. I look at the wide-open space in front of us. The woods shield the area like a fortress, secluded and mysterious. "This is where the dancing takes place and over here is the fire…" She skips over to a pit and points to an area dug into the ground. "David, do you know what Beltane means? I mean, the *actual* meaning?"

Jess tugs on me playfully and sasses back, "*Pfft*. Of course, he knows, Chloe." She stares at me. "Don't you?"

I quirk a smile and shoot a glance toward Hannah. "Bright fire," I reply, but I don't leave it at that, and add, "But, some believe it's derived from a sun god named Belenus. Would you like me to go on?"

Jess smiles like a vixen and chides Chloe, "See? He's hot as fuck *and* clever."

Chloe twirls around the pit and then kneels down. "Okay…which one of us do you think will be the May queen this year?"

"That's hard to say since I'm not part of your coven, Chloe," I state soberly. She reveals a mindful expression as if she's deciding what to say next.

"Would it help if I tell you we're from the Willowshire coven?" she questions.

I chuckle and shake my head. "It's like tellin' me you're from Bermuda. I'm not familiar with Willowshire's traditions."

"All right, maybe this will help. Our coven celebrates every season, I mean we *never* miss one. Each year we honor the gods and goddesses, of course, but this season requires that the parents choose one member from their family. Usually, it's the oldest child when they come of age. If chosen, they are crowned the king or queen. This tradition, for us, is to ensure safety and fertility for our coven. It's been this way for generations," Chloe explains. She stands and quickly brushes a few traces of dirt off. She mumbles something under her breath and then tips her head toward me. "So, you wanna guess who our parents picked, David?"

I slowly direct my gaze between all three girls. Jess and Chloe stare me down like I should be sweating bullets. But as for Hannah, she's paying no mind to what's being said. If my gut instinct is right it means Hannah is the one their parents picked. I don't want to be right because if what Chloe is saying is true, someone has been chosen for Hannah. And I'm not too thrilled with that thought. I rub at the day-old scruff on my face and work my jaw before I answer.

"Hannah," I practically whisper, climbing down the massive rock.

"Ah… he guessed it, Jess!" Chloe grumbles.

"I thought I looked older!" Jess remarks in a sullen tone.

"No. Father said I looked older!" Chloe chimes in. I spin around on my boots and eye them both.

"So, how old are you?" I ask, making eye contact with Chloe.

"Twenty-five, but you know how us witches are. I could be a hundred-and-one and just have this youth-like appearance," she laughs, flicking her hair back.

Jess yells from the rock, "How old are you, David?"

"Old enough to know better," I remark, pacing around the pit. I'm taking in the scenery, the way it has narrowed paths jutting out in different directions. How serene the main area feels but how condensed, and precarious the woods are. Dangerous cliffs and rocky terrain guard this sacred space like sentinels.

Just as I'm formulating another thought, someone asks, "What about lifemates, ever heard of them before?" I crane my head around to discover it's Hannah asking.

I make my way toward her and smile. "Yeah, I've heard of them before. Why?"

She closes her book, sends me an unsure grin, and asks, "It's not some make-believe tale, you know, like what you read in books?"

I chuckle inwardly. "Well, I can tell you they're not make-believe."

"Oh, c'mon now, don't start fillin' our sister's head with rubbish," Jess spouts, she elbows Chloe, and they erupt in laughter. *"Lifemates, Pfft!"*

Hannah waves me off as I kneel closer to her, her eyes meet mine. "Forget I asked, okay?" She rises from her seated position and I extend my hand out, she hesitates for a moment and then slips hers in mine. My fire uncoils from that deep lair within me and I caress her hand. The moment doesn't last long enough for me, and before I know it, she's standing. Our eyes never drift apart and maybe it's just wishful thinking, but there's that killer smile of hers. The one smile that could put someone in a mesmerizing daze.

"Can I have my hand back?" she laughs and gently pulls away.

"Yeah, sure," I say sounding spellbound.

She points over her shoulder and softly says, "I'm going to head back, it's getting kinda late."

I stand grounded to the earth, watching the way the slits of her dress expose her tone legs. The way her body flows with the evening breeze. I'm not a flowery printed kinda man, but I can appreciate how her dress enhances her body. A hand curls securely around my arm. "Don't worry about her, David. She just reads *way* too many books, that's all," Jess assures.

I clear my throat and reply, "Right. Well, maybe we should head back too. Remember I placed a spell on the door."

"Oh, yeah, that's right," Chloe chimes in, she eases up to my other arm and smiles. "Maybe next time we see you, you won't be so shy with your fire."

"Shy? Oh, Chloe, you haven't seen anything yet," I brashly state.

Chapter Seven

I take care of the spell on the bookstore and make my way back to the hotel intact. Hannah's sisters are a force to be reckoned with. They have no idea of the power they have combined together. I have a surprising feeling of empathy for the men they may encounter. To my disappointment, Hannah wasn't anywhere near the bookstore. Maybe she knew I'd come back. Whatever the reason, I stretch back on the hotel bed and think of her. I replay the way she looked at me, the way she spoke. She was definitely curious, but she held something back.

Evan tosses an overstuffed bag on a table and announces, "Well, the Willowshire coven has some type of weight on this town."

I prop a pillow up and make myself more comfortable. "Okay, Detective Ev, let's hear it."

"Wait…Let me guess, David. Today, you probably were in a bed somewhere, like you are now, with some woman that you'll probably never see again and snuck out while she was asleep."

"*No.* I was at a bookstore looking for the damn demon *book*—"

Evan cuts me off, "You really think the demon book will be at a bookstore, for you to just pick up?"

I lift a brow like he's absurd. "No, but I did meet Hannah and her sisters there."

Evan sits on the edge of the bed like he's unfazed by what I had just said. His back faces me as he states, "I found out there are specific rituals held at every festival, and the folks here say there's some type of agreement with the elders."

"Agreement? What does that mean?" I ask sitting up more.

Evan looks over his shoulder, his expression holds concern. "Did Hannah mention anything to you?"

"Well, her sister, Chloe, explained how they celebrate the Beltane. But she never mentioned anything about an agreement with the elders." I pause on that thought and replay her words. I cock my head to the side and add, "She said something about the parents having to choose someone from the family to play a role in the celebration."

"That's it?" he asks probing for more details.

"Oh, yeah, they're from the Willowshire coven," I nonchalantly state.

"So, they're witches?"

I nod my head. "Coven, earth elements, sacred places…uh, yeah, I think that classifies them in the witch category," I retort.

"Wait, you mean you know this for a fact, David?"

I send him a look like I'm severely annoyed and answer, "*Yeah,* they knew immediately that I was a witch in the dusty-ass bookstore. And when one of them dragged me through the woods, she showed me her element. Which, come to think of it, it wasn't that intense…" I shake my head dislodging the memory and go on. "Maybe she just didn't want to show off, but either way, Hannah and her sisters are undeniably witches."

Evan stands and starts pacing the room. "David?"

"Yeah?"

He motions a finger between us and voices gruffly, "We both decided Hannah was human the first day we saw her, remember?"

"I remember, *of course*, I remember," I mouth back.

Evan taps his temple and states each word slowly, "Demon's blood."

Hours fly by as I compare notes with Evan. The Willowshire coven may appear like a worthy coven. A majority of the members, mostly the elders, live off the grid. Each year they produce a healthy harvest enough to provide for the town. I'm guessing it helps to be an earth element in times like this. In return for this gracious offer, the inhabitants of Mistcove keep the coven's secrets. A barter pact, made centuries ago.

Mentally, I focus on a distinct picture and float it across the table and ask, "Is this the old building you had showed me? You think this is where they had made the agreement?"

Evan spins it around and flicks it back. "Yes, but unlike you, David. I wasn't as lucky to discover a harem of witches who spill some of the family's mysteries."

I rub my chin trying to put two and two together. "When did the demon book come into play?"

"Good question. We know your girls were undetectable and the only way that can happen is when someone is meddling in the book," Evan replies and leans back in his chair.

"So, this girl, Leah, you bumped into in town, told you the history here?" I ask.

"Essentially, yeah. She's the one who showed me the building and explained why there's a reasonable amount of fear everyone has of the woods." He leans over on his knees and adds, "She said the woods hold an evil no one has ever seen before, and she mentioned that some of the families here have learned how to fight against this evil."

"She's a witch?" I inquire, running a hand through my hair. Evan is the best of the best in pinpointing the Brotherhood out, but I'm becoming a little sketchy since we couldn't figure out Hannah was a witch in the beginning.

"Leah is human," he states firmly.

"And you know this…*how?*"

"She bares no crescent mark," he replies and smugly grins. "And no, David, there was no sex involved for me to discover this."

I raise my hands up. "Hey, it's not my fault that you're a G-rated kinda guy. But remember Hannah *was*—"

"Was concealed somehow, yeah, I know. So, here we have…" Evan lines notes across the table, tracing a finger over different symbols. He whispers a few words, and the images begin to glow, each one merges and changes into legible words. ***Wolfenstein***. "These were symbols etched into the building."

I jump up and adamantly tap on the table. "Now you see, Ev. I wasn't just tumbling down into a mindless fucking rabbit hole. That name means something, all of this is connected somehow."

"I get it, David. From what I understand, Leah's family owns and runs a small shop just a few blocks away from The Witchery. They sell handmade trinkets and other stuff, which is how I met her. She encouraged me to buy this…" Evan tugs on the front pocket of his jeans and slips out a ring. I take it and start inspecting it.

"What's it made of?" I ask, feeling the heavy weight of it.

"Silver," Evan replies.

I sit across from him and look closer. The band has extensive vines and roots fashioned around one another, it's extremely detailed. It looks as if the roots are pushing a snarling wolf's face toward the center.

It's so intricately designed I can't fathom the hours it would take to make something like this.

"It almost looks real," I mumble still looking it over.

"After I bought it, Leah offered to show me where the historical markers are in town. And that's when I met Hannah's parents. They own The Witchery."

"And? Did you get a vibe from them?" I question handing the ring back.

"Nothing. They seemed very normal. They asked how I was liking the town and invited us to the festival."

"You and Leah?" I ask.

"No, I told them I had a brother with me and that we're just traveling through, meeting some family a few towns away."

"Brother, huh?"

Evan raises a brow and retorts, "Would you rather I said something else?"

"Don't go there, Evan," I coldly reply. But then playfully, I place a hand over my chest and dramatically say, "You know there's nothing between us."

Evan bursts out laughing.

"C'mon, Ev. We better rest up for this shindig." I steal some of Evan's pillows from his bed and toss them over to mine. I aim a finger toward him and sternly advise, "No inappropriate touching, no handholding, not even a wink from you tomorrow, got it? I don't want Hannah getting the wrong idea...*again.*"

Chapter Eight

The wind blows an eerie breeze as Evan and I walk through town. People amble about with excitement in their eyes. Sundown is just on the horizon. Wreaths made of sycamore and hawthorn hang on every single door. All the shops and restaurants are closed for the festival, and it sets a whole other tone for the town. Altering it from a 'mystic and enchanting' to bolt-the-doors-and-hide-your-children kinda feel. We meet Leah and a couple of her friends two blocks from the hotel.

"Hey," Leah greets Evan with a blushing smile. "Um… I'm assuming this is your brother?" She extends a hand out and shakes my hand. "You guys look nothing alike," she bluntly states, and without missing a beat, she introduces her friends. Her dark hazel eyes wander back to Evan and I get the strong impression she'd much rather be alone with him.

Evan roughly pats my shoulder and reveals, "David was adopted, but I'm sure you don't want to hear all about that tonight."

Leah glances over to me and then to Evan, she lifts a tattooed shoulder and says, "All right. Um… Before we head out, I just want you to know there will be plenty of food and drinks." She smiles impishly toward Evan. "You haven't eaten yet, have you?"

Evan chuckles and replies back, "No, but I am starving." I grip Evan's arm and send a stern look toward Leah.

"You mentioned drinks there, right? Well, I hope they're nonalcoholic drinks because good ol' Evan here has been sober for about two or three years now. Right, Ev?"

Evan shoots me with a dark look but doesn't miss a beat. "Yeah, I think *you* and I both have been sober for about three years."

Leah cuts in, waving a hand like it's not a problem. "Oh, it's fine. I'm sure we can find something else for you. Besides, there will be dancing, music, a bonfire, and a little traditional thing we do, it's so much fun," she cheerfully explains. Her group of friends begin striding down the sidewalk, whispering and laughing. I've never seen a huddle of humans so eager for a witch's celebration. I note Leah hovering close to Evan, her smile grows even more each time he glances over to her.

"You know there's a lot of stories that are passed down from different families. Kinda like the one I was telling you about the other day, Evan," she announces. "But I think this one really rings true for me because my grandfather told me about it when I was younger." She points toward a steep incline. It's layered with stone steps, each one seems more fragile than the last, but as I look up, I know it's leading to the monstrous cliff above. It has to be about two to three hundred feet tall. I think back to Hannah and her sisters. They definitely knew a shorter path and I find myself somewhat impressed with how agile Jess was racing to the top. Everyone quickly forms a single line as the incline becomes narrower. Leah peeks back at us as she continues her story, "He told me this place was once called Lover's Leap. A woman had jumped off because she was so heartbroken. She was in love and when her family had told her that her lover died a gruesome death. She decided she couldn't live without him and she leaped from this very cliff to her own death. Leah pauses briefly before she adds, "The sad thing is her lover was found and he was alive."

"Well, that sucks," I remark.

Leah sends me an odd look I can't quite decipher, but then she offers Evan a small smile. "For my family, I think that's why this tradition means so much. Every season we honor the lovers by holding this celebration and metaphorically uniting the couple again. It's all in fun, of course."

Evan nods his head acknowledging her. "So, are there many tourists that attend this?" he questions. His tenor sounds genuine, but I know he's searching for more information. Inspector Ev at his finest.

"Usually there are, but not many during the winter season though," Leah replies. Gradually, we make our way to the top. Trees caress the sky as the night descends. A large bonfire crackles with life and casts out enough light that shines over the massive rock. Scents of food linger in the air and then I notice an elm tree stripped bare of its limbs. It stands upright and embellished with garlands. At the very top, it's flat like an alter or a shrine. Music hums in the background and Leah's group separates grabbing drinks and cups. Evan and I quietly scan the area.

"What do you think, David?" he voices in a low, even tone.

I rub the back of my neck, trying to look calm and casual. "There's not enough beer here for me to get drunk on."

Evan gives me a sideways glance. "Thought you were going to be our designated driver tonight."

I smirk and shake my head. "Nope, not tonight, Ev. Besides, I'm kinda wondering somethin'."

"What's that?" he replies.

"How in the hell do we know, *for sure*, that we're not standing in the heart of the Brotherhood right now?

"We don't," Evan whispers as he leans over watching Leah and her friends walk back.

"Here, I brought you this," Leah announces handing Evan a cup. She takes a sip from her own drink and gazes at him the entire time.

Devon, one of Leah's friends offers a drink to me. "I heard what you said back there, about being sober," she states brushing a strand of hair from her face. "I totally get you. So, I got your back tonight, just relax and enjoy all this shit." She winks and spins around, dramatically swaying her hips. Her red hair glistens from the fire burning a few feet away. I have a flashback of Naomi, my ex. She's the one that started this whole thing when she informed Nate and his Brotherhood followers about Alyssa. Naomi is gone now, so I erased most of the memories of her. The number one rule about our coven is you can't let other things influence you or your element. If you allow something bad, like drinking demon's blood or conjuring up a demon's book, then you're just asking for trouble. You lose that self-control and become something else. Naomi willingly sacrificed herself to the dark arts and lost. Not only her element but her life as well.

Evan pretends he's taking a drink. I eye him, and he eyes me. We observe, making sure no one is watching us, then we discreetly pour out whatever's in the cups. A couple of guys walk up, Leah amiably introduces us, "This is Greg and Malcolm." She laughs softly and proudly states, "If you *really* wanna know some good stories about this place, then Greg here is your go-to-guy. He knows all about the myths and lore of Mistcove."

Greg tilts his cup toward me and asks, "Hey, aren't you the one I saw riding through town on that Sportster? Is it custom made?"

"Yeah, it was an old Harley I had modified," I reply.

"Cool. It looks pretty aggressive. So…um, you guys came here for *this*…?" he questions as he extends his arm outward, showcasing the scene around us. Off to the side the bonfire blazes while a gathering of girls begin dancing. Their outfits are more reserved, tan leather vests with straps and buckles which sway with their movements. Even Leah and her friends are dressed in the same fashion. Most of the girls have some type of braid that layers through their hair. I'm not getting the vibe it's a sensual look they're going for tonight. I watch as Leah bounces over, she digs a ring out from a side pocket of her pants. It's similar to Evan's. She slips it on over her index finger and asks, "Do you have yours, Evan?"

Evan riffles through his pockets and finally pulls out the ring. "Yeah, I have it. You want me to put it on?"

"Uh huh," she remarks with an unwavering smile. "It's sort of the tradition for us."

Greg and Malcolm raise their hands up revealing the same ring. Malcolm studies me for a brief second and then asks, "Do you have one, David?"

"No, I forgot to swing by the shop. What was the name of it again?" I cast a glance toward Leah.

"Quicksilver Jewels and Gems," she responds with a nonchalant tone. She shrugs me off as if I'm disrupting her moment with Evan. She insistently tugs on his hand, cuts me a look and says, "Oh, well. That just means more fun for *us* tonight."

I send Evan a nod and shout, "Don't have too much fun!"

Malcolm and Greg sit their empty cups on a makeshift table. Greg brushes by me and says, "C'mon, David. Pick a girl and dance."

Devon saunters toward me. Her braids sparkle with silver as she prowls around. I dedicate some time checking her out. The skin tight pants laced with chains match her persona– tough as nails and committed to getting what she wants. "Need another drink or would you rather just stand there and gawk at me?"

I chuckle and answer, "Nothin' wrong with a man admiring a beautiful woman."

She eases the empty cup from my hand and tosses it to the ground. "Oh, yeah? Let me guess one thing about you, David?"

I lift a brow as my curiosity piques.

"You're not like most guys, are you?" she announces with a hand on her slim hip.

My smile grows. "That sounded more like a question to me," I retort. She takes my hand and entices me to follow. We trudge a path closer to the fire, intermingling with the others dancing to the beat. She shouts over the noise, "I get this feelin' there's a fire burning inside you, David." Her body rubs up against me as she moves seductively.

I lean in next to her ear and whisper, "You have no idea."

She latches her arms around my waist and sasses back, "Good, then let's just let it all go, babe, and have some fun!"

Chapter Nine

Music drowns out the sound from the hissing fire. A throng of bodies move as if hypnotized, and I can see the beads of sweat gloss over each human's face. Heart-pounding, raspy songs roll through the afterglow. The night wind coaxes hidden desires and I'm absorbed in it all. Devon twirls and whips her hair back. "That's it, David. Let it all go," she pants breathlessly running her hands through my hair. I know Evan believes they're not witches, but Devon certainly could pass off as one. Her big grey eyes pierce right through me as she shimmies down my body.

The upbeat melody dies away and the crowd splits apart making a path. Torches ignite around the giant rock that Hannah's sister had shown me. The flames spotlight the area like a barbaric medieval staging with an array of flowers and bones covering the stone. Men garbed in leather-bound hide stride up and take their positions up front. Their faces are concealed with dark hooded masks. No one moves, not a breath seeps out. A low growl ushers through the air and then a drumming pulsates through the ground. The entire feel of the place changes drastically and becomes more of a symbolic setting. A chanting arises from the hooded men as if they're calling out to the Gods. The words are encrypted and filled with a deeply rooted meaning. A woman appears, wearing a black cloak. She takes a stance ahead of the path. Her voice joins in forming a unity of sounds. The words, her tone, and the drumming blend in creating a dream-like sensation.

Out of the darkness, a couple emerges, their faces are disguised. The male is clad in black and covered in animal hide which only exposes his eyes. The female is clothed in white, wearing a veil, of sorts. It's made of leathery frayed fringes that covers parts of her painted features. As she walks by I focus on her eyes. It's Hannah. Her blue-grey eyes briefly skim over me, and I know beyond a shadow of a doubt—*it's her*.

The crowd loudly cheers as the couple takes the primeval stage. An older stocky man wrapped in a greyish fur cloak fans out smoke from a chalice. Suddenly, I can smell the vigorous scents of sage and rosewood. Others join the couple; their faces are smeared with pigment and greasepaint. Recognizing anyone like Chloe or Jess will be impossible. The older bearded man turns and blows the wispy smoke toward Hannah and then to the next shrouded figure. The drumming softens as he performs his ritual. The gathering becomes instantly hushed when he steps forward. Holding two elaborate chalices, he raises them high in the air for all to see. And then he speaks. The words may sound foreign to most, but I can easily understand the witch's words…

"Fires of the ancient, moons of light keep us safe this Beltane night.

In the hidden darkness familiar creatures' saunter.

For centuries uncounted stories have been told, of woodland animals and things of old.

For in the darkness unfamiliar creatures, too, shall wander.

Fires of the ancient, moons of light make us strong this Beltane night!"

The faint drumming becomes louder and a deep, guttural noise hums throughout. Hannah moves forward and chants. She uses no words as she sings, it's solely her tone pitching from high to low. I'm rooted to the ground. Spellbound with the sound of her voice and how the pulsating music unites. It's raw, native, and surreal and I can't tear my eyes away. It's like I'm standing in an ancient forest with runes manifesting beneath my feet. Everyone crowded around me starts dancing as if it's a primal need to let it all go. A row of men, their expressions guarded with animal hides, circle and dance around the couple. The chalices are offered to Hannah and to the man standing beside her. Each drink and hand the empty cups back. No one seems to notice, and no one seems to even care.

The men maneuver around, taking a place forward, and slam their wooden staffs into the rock. The bonfire extinguishes out leaving the scene completely darkened. A roar of laughter and complaining voices consume the blackout but then a new light shines. A rave of cheers and applauds begin as the full moon rises above the tree-line and illuminates everything below. A sudden howl and then a scream echoes through the woods, but again, no one seems to give a damn. A new song plays and stifles out the outcries. Devon sways around me, laughing as if she's stoned or intoxicated.

"C'mon, David. Dance with me," she begs tugging on my arms.

The bonfire is reignited, and flames whip out exposing the scene more. Fewer people are dancing, and as I scan the stage everyone's vanished, including Hannah. I raise my head up and look for Evan, but he's disappeared too. Leah, Malcolm, and Greg are strangely nowhere to be found for that matter. I grip Devon's arm. "Hey, where are your friends?"

"*What?!*" she yells over the pounding music.

"Your friend, Leah?" I shout.

"*Leah?*" she questions scrunching her brows together. "I don't know. Don't worry about them, David. They can take care of themselves."

I release her arm and start to move away. Devon latches on, desperately gripping my wrist. "Wait, David. Don't go." I'm getting this uncanny feeling she's trying to distract me from something.

"Look, I need to go check on my *fri—brother.*" I cast her a steely-eyed glare, but it doesn't change her attitude. "Can I have my arm back now?" I insist prying her hand away. She laughs but it's not a *girly-I'm-embarrassed* kinda laugh. Anxiously she runs her fingers through her hair and meets my eyes.

"It's not a good thing for you to be wandering around by yourself, David." Her tone is jittery and strained, yet she still tries to put on a confident expression.

She makes an attempt to look away from me, but I grip her chin and look her straight in the eyes. "Why is that?"

"*I—I* may have put something in your drink," she confesses.

I laugh inside and shake my head. Evan and I knew there would be the possibility of this which is why we tossed our drinks earlier. But what did she use and why?

I release her chin and cross my arms over my chest. "Wait. What? Were you trying to kill me or roofie me?"

"It was just a little somethin' to help liven things up a bit. I wasn't trying to… you know. *Hurt you*. It's what we all take once in a while," she rambles and hesitantly lifts a shoulder. "It was just for fun. I swear." I push by her and make sure she doesn't latch onto me.

"David, wait! You can't just leave!"

"Watch me!" I holler as I zigzag through the throng of people. My body aches to shift but I know Devon's eyes are still locked on me. I sidestep around a couple and dodge the handsy women. If it were any other night I'd be all over this, but my guard is up. Something's wrong here. My path becomes darker and more restricted as I enter the woods, but I know I'm not alone. A rustling sound resonates through the thick-set trees, and I crouch low to the ground. Someone dashes over a fallen limb and jumps on top of a rock. From their stance, I can tell it's a female as she slides a silver-tipped arrow from her leather-bound quiver. She aims holding her position with stealth and control, but before she releases, she whispers something I can't make out.

The arrow spins through the air, and as I watch, I spot the target— a wolf.

Chapter Ten

The grey wolf swerves and avoids the hit, but it doesn't discourage the archer. She positions another arrow and kneels. *Swoosh.* The arrow sails by and strikes a tree, but the wolf is long gone. I hear the voice of a male approaching, and I cloak myself. "Did you get it, Leah?"

"No, but I'm going to kill every last one of them," she states hopping down from the rock.

"Here take these," the male urges. He slips out a handful of arrows from the quiver attached to his belt. "We'll come back and get your other arrows. C'mon, we're running out of time." He turns like he's scouting the area and I realize it's Malcolm. I watch silently as they run through the woodlands. Their voices are hushed as their hunt begins. A howl rips through the air and a ruckus of noise draws my attention. I stand, still cloaked, and shift to the next cluster of trees and then I spot another wolf. This one is bigger with darker fur and leads a pack. The pack speeds over rocks and brush like it's nothing, racing toward Leah and Malcolm. I use the sliver of light from the moon and shift to where I can see.

Wolves circle a huge oak, snarling and pacing restlessly. I drag my eyes up and catch another female in the tree with an arrow poised and ready to strike. Leah and Malcolm rush in launching a stream of arrows. "Look, over there, Leah! There's the one you hit," Malcolm shouts. He aims a finger toward a jagged incline. It's covered in a trail of blood.

"Wait! You can't track it through there, it's too dark," another male declares. His clothing resembles the rest of the hunters, leather-bound straps, and armed with silver-tipped arrows. "C'mon, this way!" He jerks Leah's arm and directs her west, but she doesn't move immediately.

Instead, she eyes Malcolm with concern and asks, "Where's Greg and the others?"

Malcolm motions over his shoulder and answers, "They're coming, don't worry. We'll meet up at the lake." A second passes as if she's considering his words but then she nods, and they race off into the shadows. I'm caught in a dilemma. *Do I save the archer from the teeth-baring wolves, or hunt down the wounded wolf before the others do?* My instincts kick-in, my fire pulsates through my veins and I can't shake the impulse to chase something. Something I have no fucking idea why? It could be dead by the time I find it. It's bleeding out fast, and *if* I do find it, it's probably going to rip me to shreds because I'd be pissed off too if someone shot an arrow through me.

Shifting through the woods gives me an advantage. I'm invisible to the human eye, faster and able to cover more area. The only downside to this is I'm not sure who the good guys are, or the bad. The air becomes thick with anticipation, my fingertips twinge with fire. *Easy now.* I can't let the world know I'm here yet. Footsteps race by, voices beckon behind me and I jump down to the next ridge. The bloody trail leads straight into a cave. I spin around and touch the bloody ground. It's fresh, it has to be close. I crush the leaves damp with blood and cast a spell, *"Evanscet. Ego apstergo."* The blood dissolves and the leaves shrivel up. I then blow across my palm and allow my element to lace with it. The remnants scatter like embers over the area leaving no trace for miles away.

I skirt around the trees making sure I don't disturb anything and enter the cave. *"Flame on,"* I command using the softest tone I can. An orb of flames guides me into the unknown. I trudge deeper into muck and slime until I hear a sound. Oddly, fear doesn't play a role in my actions. Curiosity. Curiosity is what drives me to unravel what lies beyond these stone-cold walls. I stoop lower and catch a movement out of the corner of my eye. Blending in with the surroundings is a wolf lying on the ground. Soft ashen fur glistens in red, its body pants and shivers desperate for a breath. My boot slips making my presence known, and then our eyes meet. I'm stunned as I stare into those familiar blue-grey eyes. Pain, and agony override her from running from me. I skim over the body matted in blood and spot the shaft of the arrow embedded in her side.

I drop to my knees and hold my hands out. "Shh, I'm going to help. *I—Just,*" I start to say but her guard goes up. I see nothing but teeth as she snarls, warning me to back off. I have to give it to her though, she's a fighter. I drop my hands and mention one small fact, "Is this the way you wanna die? Because that's what's going to happen to you if you don't let me pull that damn thing out."

The air in the cave is damp and stagnant, but it doesn't compare to the prominent scent from the wound. I grow impatient and move closer. "Look, no flames. I'm not carrying a bow," I explain cautiously, and angle my body so she can see I'm unarmed. A moment of silence stretches between us, and then she lowers her head. Her jaw slackens, teeth no longer a problem until I grab the shaft of the arrow. It's lodged in pretty good, and I have to dig in deeper to grasp it. A growl ricochets around the cave, and I try to soothe her. "It's okay…*almost got it.*" I know it has to be tough having someone yank out a twisted broadhead from your side. Blood pours out like a river when I remove it, quickly I tear off part of my shirt and cover the gaping lesion. Her limp body dangles in my arms the second I pick her up. "*C'mon,* don't quit on me now, Hannah."

I haul ass back through the cave. "Bet you thought you could fool me, huh?" I grumble dodging the sharp overhanging rocks. "Nope. I knew it the moment I laid eyes on you," I chuckle uneasily. I'd light up the area more, but I don't want to draw attention, especially since I have her in my arms. I'm not like Marc, able to shift himself and Alyssa to safety in the blink of an eye. That was their mystification in the witch world. Their bond to each other went above and beyond most.

I'd cloak us, but that takes energy, and that energy could take anything she has left. I'm not taking any chances. I duck under a branch once we're back out, and I stop dead in my tracks.

"Evan?"

"David?"

Evan holds another limb back and lets me pass. "I thought I felt another witch out here. What are you doing?"

I send Evan a side glare. "I'm out here hunting Easter eggs." I take a few steps and turn. "What does it look like I'm doing, Evan?"

"You're carrying a wolf. Wait… why is there so much blood all over you?"

"She's been hit," I state the obvious and keep moving forward. "Where have you been?"

"In the woods looking for you, David," he retorts and shifts next to me. "You know Leah and—"

"And the others are hunting the wolves, yeah, I know." I readjust my grip and study Evan. "So, did Leah decide to give you an itinerary for tonight's event?"

"No, she never said anything to me, but I do know, if we don't hurry up we're going to have more things to worry about than a wolf on our hands." Evan cloaks himself and shifts a few feet away. He waits a beat, uncloaks, and then motions for us to follow.

"Where are we heading?" he questions using a whisper-like tone.

"The hotel," I return, observing the sudden quietness in the woods. It feels like we're being watched by someone, or *something*. Evan suddenly appears in front of me, his face shows absolute confusion. It's the first time I can say I have ever seen this look on him.

"David, are you nuts? You—*we* cannot bring a wolf inside the hotel."

I shoulder past him and taunt, "C'mon, Ev. Where's your sense of adventure?"

Chapter Eleven

"All right, we're here," Evan coolly announces as he slants his body facing me. He's obscuring the view from others as they mosey by. My jacket covers most, except maybe the tail. "I think we can make it through the lobby, pass the front desk, and to the elevator without anyone noticing."

"Or you could make a distraction," I propose and hedge around the cornerstone of the hotel. Evan's in guard mode, twisting his head back and forth monitoring between two bristly shrubs.

"Like what?"

"Act like you're wasted. Trip over something and stumble around, you know?" I pause on that thought. Evan drunk? I highly doubt it. He's like a stuffed shirt and I bet the only time he's ever been remotely close to the word *wasted* is when he was a guard for the Brotherhood. That's how they got their kicks and the intensified powers by drinking demon's blood. It's nothing compared to having an old shot of witch's brew. No. Demon's blood makes you crave for one thing… *more demon's blood.*

"David? You do realize there are other witches lingering here," he spouts before he peeks through the bushes. "It would be a dead giveaway if I were to stagger myself into the hotel." He cuts me a look like I'm a little slow on the uptake. "C'mon." Evan steps out and saunters toward the door. I cringe as I enter the main lobby, every inch of this place reminds me of an old, demented grandmother. From the yellow, stained wallpaper to the outdated porcelain lamps, but the worst of it all is the fossilized photos. Expressionless portraits of different families and even a simple man wearing his Sunday-best. They're everywhere though, and each time I stride by one of them— *It's like they have eyes watching every move I make.*

"Hey, Ev?" I hint subtly at the lady seated in the lobby. "You wanna do somethin' about that?" She's about ten feet away, flipping through a magazine, but she's not reading it. Evan mouths a few words and hits the elevator button. He reaches back like he's rubbing the stiffness out of his neck and then waves his fingers outward. It's discreet enough no one notices until the cup sitting next to her crashes to the floor. Liquid spills and the woman jumps to her feet. "Oh, no!" she exclaims and runs to get something to clean up the mess. The elevator opens and Evan and I step inside.

"Nice," I praise, but not before I send him an approving nod. "I was starting to wonder if you were getting a little rusty using your element. Water Boy."

Evan glares over to me. "It's called control, David. Ever heard of the word?"

I scoff but I *think*—"

"Wait! Hold the door, please!" someone shouts.

My shoulders tense and I grind my teeth, *this can't be happening*. We're so close to our damn room. "Shut the door, Evan," I demand forcing my tone under my breath. Before Evan has a chance to press a button or summon a spell someone dashes inside with us.

"Oh, wow. Thanks," a guy says wearing a pink shirt and skinny jeans. "Oh, my gosh. Is it hot in here?" He quickly fans himself and straightens the collar on his shirt. "Did you two just get back from the festival thingy?"

Evan cuts a tedious look toward him and offers a slight nod.

"Well, if you ask me, I think it was excessively over-the-top and absolutely ridiculous, you know? I mean a party in the woods, really? That's just creepy within itself. Now, I get the whole cozy bonfire and a drink or two—it sets up a nice little romantic feel, *but this* was like a bizarre scene from some horror movie. It was just *way* too much for my taste."

Evan grunts noncommittally and I position myself behind him.

The guy runs a hand through his thick, wavy blond hair, ruffling it, and checks Evan out. "Love your jeans, by the way, they're very fitting." Evan darts a look and I know he's thinking the same, this guy swings the other way. "So, what are you two doing? Heading in for a little nightcap maybe? I don't mean to sound nosey, but I came here with a close friend and he kinda wandered off with someone else. I'm a little heartbroken as you can tell, but you know what they say about this place. It's supposed to be filled with magic and blah, blah, blah," he rambles on and pats Evan's arm. "I think the magic part is just all for advertising, really. I mean who *honestly* believes someone can tell your future by reading the creases on your hand?" He dramatically rolls his eyes and leans over, attempting to peek my way, but Evan blocks his view.

"Uh, I'm guessing your friend over there had too many drinks? Do you need some help getting him to your room because I'd be more than happy to help? It's not like I'm doing anything—"

"I think we have it covered," Evan curtly responds.

"*Ah*…I see your friend is wearing one of those critter tails. One of those clip-on things *but* you two don't look like the type that's into cosplay. Wait a minute…*Yeah*, I see it now…" the guy props a hand along his hip and grins like he just solved a riddle. "You naughty boys, you're into that freaky-tail fetish. *Hmm*?"

The elevator dings and the door opens. I quickly slip out and head straight for our room. I don't have time to listen to his assumptions that Evan and I are getting it on with sex toys and his ghastly aversion for the woods. I can still hear Evan and his unwanted companion conversing out in the hall as I make my way toward one of the beds. Once I have Hannah down, I remove my jacket and check her wound. The soft, silver-like fur has streaks of dried blood, but I'm not finding the gash where the arrow hit. Hannah's still unconscious. She hasn't moved a muscle since I moved her from the cave.

"Demon's blood," Evan states as he closes the door. He edges up next to me and motions toward her. "Whoever you think this is, had demon's blood tonight. The injury has probably healed already."

I face him and ask, "You sure?" A tiny piece of doubt riddles through me, but if I know anything about Evan, he's on-target when it comes to demon's blood.

"I'm sure, David. I knew the scent as we were leaving the woods." He steps away and rummages through a brown duffle bag. "Here, you better put this on," he says, tossing me a clean t-shirt. "I think that's what was in the chalices."

"Why? Did you get your hands on some?" I question tugging on the clean shirt and trashing the other.

"No, but everything seemed to change when they drank from them. None of the humans even noticed it. Except for Leah and her friends like they were waiting for the right moment to strike."

"So, what is it? A hobby for them?"

Half-heartedly Evan chuckles as he hands me a washcloth. "I don't think *hobby* is an adequate word here. It's more of retaliation between the families."

I scrub my hands and face as I watch him in the mirror. The slightest whiff of demon's blood can trigger a relapse. Causing some to spiral back into that addictive hunger, a hunger that can kill and I don't want Evan anywhere near the stuff. As much as I hate to admit it, though, he's right about having *control,* and he has a shit-ton of it. He dominates that ball and chain.

"Okay," I reply drying off. "So, in this so-called festivity, we have a full moon, wolves, and a feud between families. Am I right?"

He walks over to the desk opposite of the beds and takes a seat. "I believe we're going to get our answers when she wakes up," he remarks. "Why do you think this is Hannah?"

"I never said I thought it was."

He narrows his dark eyes at me. "You wouldn't have brought her back here if you thought it wasn't her, David."

I sit on the edge of the bed and glance back at her. *What if I'm wrong? What if—fuck the what ifs.* "I saw her eyes, it's her," I state. My voice carries no hint of skepticism.

"What if you're wrong?"

"What if I'm not?" I counter.

Evan leans back in the chair and stretches out his legs. "I guess time will tell."

Chapter Twelve

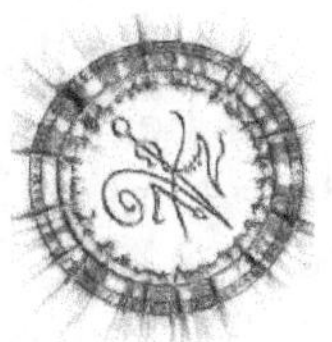

In the morning, the sun glistens through the blinds of the hotel room. My head droops forward, the sudden motion has me pop my head back up. "Glad to see you decided to join us, David. Dreaming about fire and brimstone this time?"

"What?" I ask in a grating voice. My mind drifts with fragments of wolves and arrows and then I snap out of it. "Where's Hannah?" Jumping to my feet I pivot around. My eyes fall to the empty bed.

Evan throws a thumb toward the bathroom. "She's in there. We need to find some clothes for her."

I peer over to him. "She's naked?"

Evan stands and grabs his jacket before he walks toward the door he says, "Yes, apparently whenever they change, their clothes are useless, shredded and torn from the transformation. And just so you know, David. Her wound has completely healed." He watches me for a beat, studying my expression. I know what he's thinking, we've found our lead. The one thread that could show the way to the book. Evan's pretty good at hiding his emotions but the cocksure look in his eyes exposes everything. He knows she's had demon's blood and he has his validation now.

He leaves without saying another word.

Hannah steps out of the bathroom, wrapped in a bedsheet. She's just as beautiful as the first time I saw her. Locks of goldened hair fall past her bare shoulders, no sign of dirt or blood touch her and I'm more captivated by her sheer, natural beauty. She takes a seat in a chair across from me, gripping the sheet close to her chest. "So, um…did your friend leave?"

I lower myself, sitting on the edge of the bed. "Yeah, he's going to find some clothes for you."

She glances away from me as if she's embarrassed. "Thanks for helping me last night."

I comb my fingers through my hair and casually reply, "No problem. Is there anything else I can do?"

Her eyes lock onto mine and I feel this urging need from her. "Leave," she voices in a tone that's almost threatening. But her eyes are telling me an entirely different story.

I sit up straighter and cock my head to the side and ask, "Leave the room?"

"No, Mistcove. This…" she pauses as her eyes drift nervously from mine and presses on, "This town isn't what you think it is."

I lean over on my knees. "I know what you are. I know what you're capable of and right now I don't give a fuck about this town. I only want to help you, Hannah."

"That's not true, David. You're here for a book," she retorts and stares at me like I'm a hypocrite.

"Your friend, Evan, pretty much interrogated me about the witches, the coven, and a book. So, you can stop pretending you care."

I shake my head and raise my brows irked that she'd even think for a second that I'm using her. "You can ignore, Evan. He's wary of people and you can't blame him because after last night's celebration. I'd say things took a turn for the worst."

"If you were a human then you would have never known how things really are," she states evenly.

I chuckle, "Yeah, sweetheart. Maybe that's true but lucky for you, I'm not."

"So, what is it you want?"

I ease back and fold my hands in my lap and smile. "There's a lot of things I want, but what I really want is your time, Hannah. Maybe you could explain why Leah and her pals were on a hunting spree?"

She takes in a heavy sigh and lets a moment pass between us. "Our coven is cursed. You see, long ago in my family, Wolfenstein, a young witch fell in love with a human. And as you know, this is forbidden for our kind, but nevertheless, the two continued their love affair for some time. Until one day when he met another and ended their relationship. From that point, Luna went mad with vengeance, but not toward the humans. Instead, she filtered her rage toward her own and cursed us. For centuries, with each full moon, we have changed into fully-formed wolves. We think, we act, we behave as if we were born a wolf. And along with this curse our own earth element diminishes. It was the sacrifice she gave up to invoke the hex."

I lower my eyes from her and soak in her words. "So, your element has been weakened?"

"Let's just say, I have never known what it's like to use my element completely. I mean we have it, it's there, but from what I've read earth elements are known to enhance a forest, grow an abundance of plant life or even move the terrain around them. The only practical thing we're able to do is produce a decent amount of crops."

I click my tongue and think back to the barter pact. Pieces start to fall into place and then my next question emerges. "Okay, so what's up with Leah and her crew?"

She shakes her head lightly and replies, "I'm sure you've heard the story of Lover's Leap by now. One of Mistcove's legacies where the woman jumps from the cliff because she was heartbroken. Well, that woman happened to be Leah's great-great-aunt, and the man she thought died was part of our coven. Her family knew what he was and believed the only way to stop their relationship was to tell her he had died, but no one expected her to take her own life. So…for many years they have hunted us."

I watch her intently, watching the way her emotions play across her face and I see a candidness riddled with uneasiness. The curse and the story show me a different perspective, but it doesn't quite explain everything. I lick my lips and rub my chin thinking about the book and wonder why would anyone want to call on the dark arts? "All right, let me get this straight. Your coven was cursed many moons ago, and you have a group of leather-bound humans hunting you down like it's some type of sport." I have so many other questions I want to ask her, but only one stands out above the rest.

"So, where's the book, and is there someone you know that has it?" I question.

"Like I told your friend, I have no idea about the book you're looking for," she responds sternly. My view switches from her face when she stands, a hint of her thigh exposes and my eyes race over her. The thin sheet outlines the curves of her body perfectly, every inch of her screams, *touch me, David.* Toned, fair-skinned and legs that could go on for days, but before my body fully catches up with my brain I hear…

"David? How much longer will your friend be?"

"Am I not good company?" I tease and place a hand over my chest. "I'm hurt and just when I thought we were becoming friends."

She stands beside the window, peeking through the blinds. "David, stop it. I have to go home before they send out a search party for me." She glances back and reveals a timid smile. "Besides you're not the one wearing hardly anything," she says tugging on the white sheet.

My smile grows. "Hey, I'm not complaining."

"Of course not," she responds.

There's something about a woman when she blushes, the way her cheeks flush with a whisper of red, and her breathing accelerates. My mind wanders— what would it be like to have her beneath me, panting, moaning my name, and then her voice pulls me from my carnal thoughts.

"I know what you're thinking."

"Oh, yeah?" I stand and slowly walk toward her. "And what would that be?" I question brushing a strand of hair off her shoulder. We're so close I can feel each breath she takes, and I take the moment and observe the way she looks at me. Is it lust in her eyes? No, there's something else etched in her. She sways on her feet and I grip her arm. "You okay?"

"Yes. I…um," She hesitates briefly and looks down. "You think I'm lying, about the book, don't you?" she asks softly and then gradually her eyes find mine.

"I don't know if you are, but right now there's only one thing on my mind," I reply in a husky tone. My hand coasts along her arm, her neck, and up to her chin. She closes her eyes as if she's savoring my touch, and then I lean in to kiss her. I take my time relishing the softness of her lips, the sweet, tempting taste of her, and then the door opens.

"David?" Evan calls out, striding into the room. I don't move and she doesn't either, it's like we're both locked in a spell. The fire in me heats my flesh, and I have no idea if she knows the effect she has on me until she sucks in a sudden breath. My hand still cradles her chin delicately as if I'm grasping the most valuable riches in the world.

"David?!" Evan barks, his tone is harsher as he attempts to get my attention.

Slowly, I turn and face him. "Yeah?"

"I have her clothes. They're probably not the exact size, but I think they'll work," he says placing them down on the bed.

My hand falls from her face as she moves away from me. "Thank you. I'm sure whatever you brought will be fine," she announces and rushes toward the bathroom to change.

Evan steps up and sharply whispers, *"What are you doing, David?"*

I send him a glare. "What do you mean?"

"I mean that we don't know if she's the one conjuring the demon, David. She has its blood running through her veins," he growls. "How else would she recover so quickly from last night, hmm?"

I glance briefly toward the bathroom making sure we're both alone and retort, "We don't know enough to make that kind of judgment, Evan."

He scoffs. "This isn't a game of kiss and tell, you know? The Brotherhood are deceptive in every way and just because you think she's beautiful and has a great pair of legs doesn't change anything."

I point my finger in his chest. "See, I knew you were jealous."

The floor creaks and we both turn our heads and find Hannah standing just a few feet away. "I think I'm going to go now," she announces somberly. "Thanks again for everything," she says making a beeline toward the door.

"Hannah, wait," I assert, my tone carries across the room sounding demanding and rough. I don't know how much she heard but I don't want her leaving here with some preconceived notion. "Look, my buddy and I are not going to hurt you," I state and slap the back of my hand against Evan's chest. "Right, Ev?"

"No, that's not our intent. We just want some answers, Hannah," Evan explains and sidesteps around me.

She studies us, her eyes darting between me and Evan. "I already explained everything to you. What more do you want?"

"The truth," Evan boldly states. "How did you heal so quickly from the arrow that hit you last night?"

She takes a defiant step back and tucks a strand of hair behind her ear. "You don't know what our coven has been through. The measures we've had to take to stay alive, but if you're trying to suggest we've somehow harnessed a demon by using a book then you're wrong. My father has crafted many elixirs to help us, to *save us* from the very thing that happened last night. So, you can take your accusations and shove them where the sun doesn't shine because I'm done with this."

"Hannah!" Evan and I both shout in unison but it's too late. She leaves slamming the door loudly behind her.

"Well, that didn't go as I expected," Evan remarks staring at the door.

I raise my brows. "Really? What did you think would happen with you grilling her over the fucking book?"

"I needed to know, David," he states and motions a finger in-between us. "*We* needed to know. We have to know what we're dealing with."

Softly I chuckle. "You're one of the few men I know that has no tact with women."

Evan plops down on one of the beds and cuts me a look. "Oh, so seducing women is the key then, is that it?"

I wave him off. "I wasn't trying to seduce her."

He laughs. "That's not how it looked from where I was standing."

"Yeah, well she was already hot and bothered by me that day at The Witchery."

Evan smirks and lightly shakes his head. "Hot? I believe it was more like *bothered*, David."

I jerk my jacket on and ignore him. "C'mon, Detective smartass. We have a book to find."

Chapter Thirteen

I knew Hannah would be long gone after our little discussion earlier. Who in their right mind would want someone interrogating the fuck out of them? Plus, the clothes Evan so gracefully bought, made her look like a groupie from the 1970s. A psychedelic poster girl with a *peace-and-love* sign printed boldly on the front of the tie-dyed shirt. Maybe it was his subliminal way to show her we're not the bad guys. Either way, she definitely caught me off-guard to see her stand up to us. On the same note, it kinda turned me on. She's got spunk I'll give her that.

Evan sends a message to my phone saying he's found Malcolm and that he'll get back with me later. I slide my cell into my back pocket and suddenly feel like I'm being watched. A couple passes by staring, keeping their distance from me. I scan the streets and decide to head toward the coffee shop. This town relies heavily on the old ways. Everything is handcrafted, the foods are made from scratch and nothing reveals the secrets that dwell within. Unless, that is, you know what to look for.

My next destination is the hidden bookstore. Hannah wasn't at The Witchery, one of the waitresses had told me she had taken the day off. The usual ladies were there, sending me their friendly smiles. But it's not their subtle waves and pleasant smiles that throw me off— it's this needling sensation that they know something I don't.

I follow the same path down the narrow alleyway and into the darkness. A quick snap from my fingers and I have flames guiding me, but as I reach the bottom there's no entryway. Bricks conceal the way in. I glide my other hand over the wall and sense a different spell has been cast. Annoyed, I work my jaw and pivot around, searching for another way in. After meticulously hunting, I find nothing and face the entrance I know is there. I let out a huff, stretch my neck from side to side, and focus on the spell. The energy connected to it is strong, but if I can find a weakness then I can revoke it.

Carefully, my fingertips skim along the artificial bricks. Inch by inch I explore the characteristics of each surface. I stoop lower until I feel it. One of the bricks shrinks away from my hand. *"Found it,"* I whisper to the dark. Pressing hard on the area and maintaining my stance I summon a spell. "Ego mandatum vos ut revelare ipsum. Ego quaerere praetervecto. Sic fiat semper." The air around me swirls, hushed voices intermingle as if our spells are clashing together. I decide to take it to the next level and ignite my fire. Bright red flames outline the door, and I can see inside. Determined I repeat my words with more strength,

"Ego mandatum vos ut revelare ipsum. Ego quaerere praetervecto. Sic fiat semper." Gradually the facade of stone tumbles to the ground as my fire renders it free.

I shake off my hands, letting the last tendrils of flames die out, and walk inside. The smell of old books overcome me, the lighting seems more somber and I delay my next step. "Hello? Anyone here?" The first time I entered it felt somewhat cozy, tranquil even. But now it's as if I've stumbled into a neglected basement filled with books that's been long forgotten. The lanterns still hang emitting an eerie glow on each wooden shelf. I resume my stride, passing quietly through the darkened aisles. A woman's laughter flows like silk through the room and then another echoes back. "Knock, Knock," I announce tapping my knuckle against a shelf. Each step becomes slower as I move through the store. Not a sound ushers back as I peer around the next corner. I make my way to the third set of bookshelves and feel a breath along my neck.

"Who's there?" the breath whispers.

I halt my movements and listen. Distant voices banter back and forth but their words are too vague to understand. I rap my knuckles again on the next shelf and reply, "Witch."

"Witch who?" a seductive voice questions.

"Which one of you will reveal yourself to me?" I ask.

"Depends," a softer voice whispers back.

"On?" I prod moving forward. Each time I feel like I'm getting closer to them, I realize they shift away. Leaving me in the dark.

"Can you keep a secret?" the first sensual voice beckons.

"Yeah," I slowly draw out.

A book pushes forward and collapses to the floor beside my boots. I bend down and pick it up and then look at where the book came from. In between the other tomes shines a slither of light and as I peer in— I see Hannah across the dimly lit space.

"She likes you," the softer voice whispers, and then I sense a finger lightly trail along my lips and down to my throat. I turn and face Chloe. Her sky-blue eyes twinkle with delight as she taps a finger to her own lips. "*Shh*, it's our little secret, okay?"

I give her one of my prominent smiles and answer, "All right."

"Did he promise, Chloe?" Jess questions, her tone carries a wariness. My eyes follow her as she removes another book exposing the other side of the aisle.

Chloe lifts a shoulder. "More or less."

Jess' brows scrunch together as she leans in on the shelving. "How did you break the spell?"

"No, wait, I want to know if we scared you? Did we?" Chloe chimes in, her grin widens by the second. "Oh, gosh. I love it when you smirk like that, David. Can you see it, Jess? I told you he has this racy look about him."

Jess eases in closer and mutters, "It's not just his smirk, Chloe. It's all of him. I mean look at him, look at those clover-green eyes and his thick dark hair, which by the way, I'd love to run my hands through."

Chloe snags the book from my hands and tosses it over to a different shelf. "How did you break the spell, David?"

I offer one of Chloe's favorite smirks and raise a hand upward. A sphere of fire spins around in the middle of my palm. "Sometimes you have to use a little fire to remove a stump."

"You better not say that to Hannah," Jess remarks as she glances over her shoulder making sure Hannah is still busy with her stack of books. "You've just broken her best spell. Her *do not disturb spell*." She tips her head like she's in disbelief.

Chloe pushes her sleeves up and mumbles something to Jess through the small open space in the bookcase. They remind me of two informers laying out some kind of cryptic plan shrouded within the shadows. Chloe whispers first to me, "Remember the secret I told you?"

"Ah, yeah?" I respond wondering if she thinks I have some kind of short-term memory.

"Well, there's a problem because if you…" Jess grimaces like whatever she's about to say grosses her out but goes on, "like her too, but I don't *really* see the attraction between you two. I mean look at her." She angles her body back a bit so I can get a view of Hannah. I see legs mostly as she stands on a stepping-stool arranging things on a higher shelf. She's in shorts and a pale blue top, it fits her better than the flower-child getup Evan had brought her. "She's plain and boring. All she needs is a pair of black cat-eye glasses and you'll have it— Nerdville." Jess and Chloe laugh quietly to themselves.

"And you have Silas. I'm sure you saw him at the festival, David," Chloe adds cheerfully. Jess pokes a book at Chloe urging her to go on. "He was the king." She lifts a hand and pretends she's measuring my height. "Yeah, Jess. I think they have the same build."

"I remember, and I also recall a group of humans chasing down a pack of wolves, too," I return, and watch the two bicker back and forth.

"She told him. I just know she did," Chloe grumbles.

"I know I would tell him all my dirty little secrets if I spent the night in his bed," Jess admits and peeks through the gap.

"We should've confronted her this morning when she was sneaking out of the hotel," Chloe whispers and hunches lower, ducking for cover as Hannah changes her position. The sound of the metal stool clangs and squeaks while she folds it up.

"We should have, but we didn't," Jess mumbles between leather bound pages.

They both let out an exasperated sigh and then Chloe's face brightens. "I have it. David, we would like for you to come to dinner at our place tonight," she states energetically.

"Dinner?" Jess questions.

I'm getting from Jess' expression this is not one of their well thought out plans. I shrug and reply, "Sure, why not?"

"You sure?" Jess asks as a smile surfaces.

"Yes, he's sure," Chloe hisses back at her sister. Unspoken words linger between the two and then Chloe mentions, "Hannah's not going to be very happy about this, but you'll be our guest, okay?"

I cock my head to the side and curiously ask. "Why would this upset Hannah?"

Jess pipes in, "Hannah has a weakness."

"Yeah, a weakness," Chloe repeats shaking her blonde head up and down.

"Is this another secret?" I ask leaning on the bookshelf.

The sisters both glance at each other briefly and then Jess whispers, "You saw the wolves?"

I jester a silent, *yes,* and whisper, "I know Hannah was one of them."

The girls eyeball each other like I'm announcing some groundbreaking news.

"He knows," Chloe asserts.

"He knows," Jess parrots back.

I raise a brow fully entertained by their antics. Chloe drags her eyes away from Jess and asks, "You know what we are then?"

"Pretty much. So, what's this weakness with Hannah?" I nod in her direction. It's clear Hannah didn't tell her sisters about last night or our conversation. For whatever reason, her lips are sealed. I move my fingers persuading Chloe to tiptoe closer. "C'mon now. Don't tease me."

She places one hand on the bookshelf and the other over her chest. "Oh, gosh, David. I would never tease you." As her body nears, her lips part and she begins disclosing Hannah's vulnerability, "You're aware wolves can run fast, especially so in short bursts, but Hannah's known to run faster than any one of us. She's never been caught or marked by an arrow which is one of the reasons she was presented as queen for this season. Our father says this virtue could also be her greatest weakness because she runs from everything—including love."

Jess mimics Chloe's serious tone and mouths, *"She runs from everything."*

I wipe a hand over my mouth, hiding a grin.

Jess yanks out another book and asks with a concerned expression, "Should we let Hannah know about our dinner proposal?"

Chloe whips back her blonde hair over a shoulder and replies, "Yes. I think we should." She stands up straighter, fixes the crocheted bow on her dress, and links her arm through mine. We make eye contact as she leads me around the corner. "C'mon, David. This shouldn't take long."

Jess is hot on our heels, keeping in step with us, she boasts, "I'll give it five minutes, tops."

Chloe snickers confidently back, "Two."

Hannah's sitting on the floor rummaging through a box. She's submerged completely in the countless things inside. Carefully, she wipes off the cover of a red bound book and blows the dust from it. Without looking up she says, "I'm almost finished." She slips a thread of hair behind her ear and stands. "Did you know this book is over a hundred years old and that its about—" The book plummets to the floor with a deafening thud. Her wide eyes pierce through me. "How did *he* get in here?!"

Chloe hugs my arm tightly. "He broke the spell," she gloats and sends me a brisk glance. "Isn't that impressive?"

Hannah promptly grabs the book from the floor and shakes her head. "No. It's not."

Jess calmly strolls by us and starts pretending she's organizing the boxes. "I happen to think it's kinda notable that he could—"

"I don't care what you two think," Hannah cuts in and clutches the book closely as if it's a barrier between her and me. Her eyes soften but her body stays as stiff as a board. "*I—I'm* supposed to keep these two out of trouble, but apparently, I'm lacking in that department." She throws a menacing glare toward Chloe and Jess.

Chloe rubs my arm. "David's no trouble, Hannah. Matter of fact, we've invited him to dinner with the family tonight," she explains with a bit more enthusiasm than needed. Hannah stands paralyzed for a second or two, mouth gaping as if the announcement devastates her.

I clear my throat. "Look, if you wanna know how I broke your spell," I offer and open my hand. I envision a book floating in the center of my palm and let my natural born element engulf it. Flames brighten and sway and then I make a fist. Smoke slips through my fingertips. "I just used my fire, no biggie." Hannah blinks and then spins around and rushes toward another room.

Jess strolls up. "Wait for it…"

Bang! A door slams shut.

Bang! Something topples over and then another loud bang rings out.

"Okay, I think she'll cool off in the next hour or so," Jess states and pats my chest.

I give Chloe a quizzical look and ask, "What?" What did I do besides break her spell?"

She bobs her head agreeing. "Yeah, that and you just displayed a burning book. So, yeah, she's pissed."

"*Fuck*," I hiss.

Chloe smiles sweetly and begins walking toward the entrance. "You did good, David. Now, let's see how you do with the family."

Chapter Fourteen

Back at the hotel, I shower and shave and berate myself for visualizing a burning book. What the fuck was I thinking? It wasn't one of my brightest ideas. Hannah probably thinks I'm insulting her and it's the furthest thing from my mind. I drag my fingers through my damp hair and sift through the sigils Evan has out and try to remember if I saw one at the bookstore. Nothing resembles any of them. I grind my teeth and pace. Hannah mentioned elixirs that helped her heal, what if she's telling the truth? Her sisters seem somewhat normal, flirty, and upbeat, but there's never been a hint of demon blood in them. No black, menacing eyes or a surge of unexplainable energy. But then again, Dean, a member from the Brotherhood bared no signs. He was able to blend in with the humans and date a human girl. As fate would have it he met his demise summoning the Demon known as Jinn one last time.

I slide a white button-up shirt on and glance in the mirror. Tonight will either go to shit or I'll get lucky and find something tangible. I scroll through my phone checking messages and note nothing from Evan yet. Evan carries the term *badass* all on his own, and I'm sure whatever he encounters he'll be fine. I've seen him slay a few Brotherhood guards and take on Jinn in battle. He may come off as reserved and standoffish, but he's also someone I'd pick first to fight along with if things went south. I tuck in the shirt, grab my jacket hanging over a chair and head out. Chloe gave me an address to follow and as I ride, passing many roads, I realize their home is closer to the lake than I had thought.

One main house sits beside the water and nestled in the woods are cabins. Twelve cabins that look almost identical, rustic, and simple. The backdrop showcases the mountains and a vivid afterglow as the sun sets below. I get off my bike and take in the scene. I get maybe five seconds to take it all in before Chloe charges out of the front door. "You came," she exclaims with a smile. She's wearing denim jeans, which I think is the first time I've seen those on her, and a peach colored shirt. She twirls around as her blue eyes widen with excitement. "Do you like it?" Flipping her braided hair back. "I had my mother help fix it for tonight. She usually does all our hair, but I think next time I can do it myself." She rocks back on her heels as she inhales a breath. "David?"

"Yeah?" I reply.

"You haven't said anything yet," she states gazing at me.

"That's because you haven't stopped talking since he got here, Chloe," Jess counters sauntering toward us. She brushes Chloe off to one side, and I can tell she's sizing me up. "You look handsome this evening, David," she says rising up on her toes, she takes a long heady sniff. "Sandalwood, cedar and—"

"Sage," Chloe interrupts, she takes my hand and escorts me toward the house. "You'll have to excuse my sister. She's not used to a lot of men here that wear cologne."

"*Pfft*... and you'll have to excuse my sister, David. She has no clue what a man really is like," Jess spouts and follows us inside. The sisters cast ugly looks toward each other and then we enter the living room area. "Mother, our guest is here!" Jess shouts.

"Here, do you want to take a seat?" Chloe asks taking my jacket and lays it on a chair nearby. "She's probably in the kitchen." I glance around the furnishings, an assortment of wide-ranging antiques coupled with the natural wood offers a cozy, warm feeling. Oil lanterns enhance the lighting which shine on a hand carved coffee table. Various plants line the windowsills and *some,* I can tell, are not what a sweet, little old lady would grow. There may be a few ferns and lilies but the hemlock and the wolfbane stand out like alarm bells.

"What are we having for dinner," I ask touching the ivy that drapes along the sides.

"Wild braised boar and beetroots," a fair-haired woman announces. I turn and catch the resemblance of Hannah, same eyes, same delicate facial structure but older. She cleans her hands off with a kitchen dishrag and smiles. "I hope you're hungry. We've made plenty," she says and motions for me to follow her.

Chloe whispers in my ear as we make our way into the dining area. "Our mother's name is Catherine."

The room wasn't much bigger than any other part of the house. Comfortable and inviting in a down-home kinda way. A stone fireplace crackles with life as an iron kettle steams above, and I smell the scent of chamomile tea brewing. Catherine moves around the table placing white speckled plates and silverware in their rightful places. "Take a seat wherever you feel comfortable, David," Catherine says in a warm tone. "Except this one, this is Elijah's seat." She taps a wooden chair stationed at the head of the table. She steals a moment and readjusts her hair that's tied tightly into a bun. "We don't get many visitors here," she modestly says. "Well, I'm sure you can understand we don't mingle with the humans much, and especially, the boys that try to curry favor with the girls. We've always protected our girls and we have to tend to our kind. I'm sure your parents did the same for you," she pauses and peers over to Chloe and Jess impatiently. She claps her hands and orders in a hushed tone, "Girls, why are you two still standing there? Go tell your sister it's time to eat."

"Where's Grandmother Greta?" Chloe insistently asks but her mother shoos them away like they're a nuisance. Catherine tidies up the table a bit more and glances at me. "Would you like to meet Grandmother Greta?"

"I would love to," I reply and let Catherine show me the way to the kitchen. She leads us through a close-knit hall covered in crawling green vines and into a spacious kitchen. I'm instantly hit with the aroma of freshly baked bread.

"Mother, he's here," Catherine announces to an older woman that's hunched over an open stove. She's wearing oven mitts as she pulls out a golden loaf of bread. I can sense her smile before she even looks at me.

"The witch boy, Chloe and Jessica are always cooing over. Ah, yes, it's finally good to see you after all the fuss you've been a causin'," Grandmother Greta voices in a flattering tone. She sets the bread pan gently down on the countertop and slides off a mitt and eyes me. Grey eyes slowly scan me from head to toe and then back up. "Fire, is that what burns through your veins? That's what the girls say anyway," she croons with a chuckle.

I return with my own chuckle and reply, "If that's what they say, then I guess it's true."

"Well, then you could've helped bake the bread." She turns away and situates the bread onto a white serving platter and then hands it to me. "Come along, David. Let's gather the food and watch the show." As we walk back into the dining area a knock clatters at the front door.

Catherine sweeps in from behind me. "I'll get it, you two finish settin' up the table," she says, tossing her words over a shoulder. Her demeanor's like she's juggling a hundred things at once. I catch Greta passing by me as she softly hums to herself, fine-tuning the dishes. Her silver-like hair is as neat as a pin, and just like her grandmotherly attire, she's composed and calm. I avert my gaze and regard the guests upfront. Two boy-ish men enter, one with red hair and the other with tawny colored hair.

"Oh, I didn't know you were bringing a friend, Silas," Catherine says and invites them in.

"I hope it's no trouble. Finn and I were planning on hanging out later and I kinda thought maybe we could catch a bite to eat," the red-haired male explains. He adds a touch of shyness to his grin.

Catherine quickly shakes hands with Finn, it's not the way humans greet, it's a coven handshake. A subtle use of magick entwines and briefly exposes they're part of the same coven. "Yes, no trouble at all. Come on in, the food is probably getting cold." She begins making her way back and smiles with a little more force. "Better find your seats before Elijah gets here."

I set the bread down and grab a chair closest to me as Catherine counts heads. "One, two, three, four, five…" She contorts herself while looking down the hall and around the room. "Where's the girls and uncle Elroy?" Her cheerful behavior soon changes to fretfulness as she nervously tugs on the round button on her dress. As she hastily exits the room, Chloe and Jess enter through the backdoor, and then a scraggly man joins the table.

"Uncle Elroy, you're cutting it kinda close, don't you think?" Jess scolds, she quickly sits in the chair Chloe pulls out.

"Hey! I was going to sit there, beside David," Chloe protests. Jess leans around me with an unconcerned expression.

"Looks like there's still a chair open on the other side," Jess points out. Chloe's entire body slumps as she rolls her eyes like a disappointed child.

"Yeah, and I'll be sitting next to mother too," she whines. Regardless of the inconvenience, she takes a seat. I fiddle with my fork while Greta and Elroy sit on the other side. Finn takes his time settling in, restlessly folding, and unfolding a napkin, and then places it near his plate. He keeps his head down low, his hair hangs over his callow features. I can understand his edginess simply because he's sitting directly in front of the girls' father. Elijah has a full view of everyone at the table as he positions himself upfront. The grandmother gives me a cordial nod, shuffling different dishes along, making sure everyone gets a hefty portion. There's only one chair vacant between Silas and Elroy. As everyone begins scooping food onto their plates Hannah appears. She's in a green apple colored dress. If she's going for a Mother Teresa kinda look, then she's nailed it. It reveals absolutely nothing. A series of large white buttons line the collar all the way down to the bottom. It's a floor length dress, but she's still hauntingly beautiful. I watch her intently as she slips into her chair and so does everyone else.

The growing tension alone could probably suffocate an army of men while drinks are being filled. Catherine is the last to finally rest her feet, a beat passes as if we're waiting for something to happen, and then it does. Elijah drums his long, neglected fingernails along the tabletop as if he's pondering the scene before him. He's well built for his age with a peppered grey beard and hard, crafty eyes. His backwoodsman appearance is vastly different than Mr. Worthington. Two very different demeanors when comparing them as high priests. Daniel Worthington's power infiltrates a room immediately. Elijah's sneaks up on you slowly and progressively. I know he's watching me as I take a drink and then he swings his glare over to Finn.

"I see here we have a few more guests this night," Elijah abruptly says.

Catherine quickly swallows her drink down and smiles. "Yes, Silas brought over one of his friends, Finn. You remember Finn and his family? They own the shop on Arbor street…"

Elijah nods and leans an arm on the table. "How's business doin', Finn?"

Finn looks up, making every attempt to look collected and replies, "We're doin' real good. Dad says if the cash flow does well next year we might just buy that land north of here." He takes a breath and adds, "You know, maybe have it for some huntin' ground?" Finn dashes an offhanded look toward me, and then back to Elijah.

Elijah inhales deeply and nods again. "Well, that's good to hear. All right, let's give our blessings."

Everyone hushes as Elijah splays his hands outward. "Oh, mighty Gods and Goddesses, may we ask of you to bless this table. Bless this bountiful food we are about to eat. May it bring strength and nourishment. We honor thee and may the spirit live within us."

As bowls and platters are busily moved around, Jess nudges me and asks, "Can you hand me the bread?" I think twice about moving the bread with my abilities, unsure how Hannah's father would react. Chloe slices a piece off and hands over the tray, her eyes linger over me. I can tell she's just on the verge of saying something, but then Elijah intervenes.

"The girls tell me, David, you're just passin' through," he says taking a bite of food.

I rest the fork in my hand and answer, "Yeah, my brother and I were on our way to meet some family."

"Your family live close by?" he questions. He dabs a portion of bread along his plate soaking up some of the juices from the braised boar.

"No, they live farther south of here."

"I take it both your parents are still alive, what do they do?" Elijah digs in deeper with queries as he chews on another slice of soused bread.

I clear my throat and reply, "They have their own medical practice. It makes a decent living for them and they seem to like it."

"So, what do you do?"

Jess moves forward bond squeezes my wrist. "He travels," Jess proudly offers and eyes me. "Isn't that right, David?"

Before I have a chance to answer Chloe jumps in with, "He's not like most around here, he's smart and charming and—"

"Are you sayin' I'm dumb, Chloe?" Silas pipes in. His shaggy red hair falls over one eye, he huffs at the wayward strand while waiting for Chloe's return.

"Dumb as dirt," she says smiling.

Silas laughs and counters with, "You wish you were as smart as me, Chloe."

"Do I?" she quips back.

As Silas and Chloe go back and forth I search across the table. Hannah meets my gaze briefly. She looks away like she's doubting herself, but then, she slowly looks back. If an electrifying force were visible it would be bold and bright threading between us. Everything around me disintegrates and I pay attention to the way her hair cascades along her shoulders. I follow up to her lips and smile inside remembering our fleeting kiss. Every second becomes harder to restrain myself. I wanna just get up, walk over, sweep her in my arms and leave. In my mind I see it all unfold and she sees it too because I watch as she smiles. How can she send me hot and cold vibes in a matter of minutes? I've seen her weak and vulnerable inside a damp, dusky cave needing to be protected. I know she can change into an entirely different form than the womanly figure she's in now, and none of it makes me want to run the other way.

"David?" a voice calls out to me.

"Yeah," I breezily reply not really knowing who's talking to me.

Jess bumps her arm against mine. "You want any more potatoes?"

I glance down, the only thing I've eaten surprisingly are the potatoes. I twirl the fork around my fingers and say, "No, I'm good. Thanks."

Chloe leans in, chewing away on her food. "Maybe tomorrow you could come back. Jess and I were thinking of taking the boat out on the lake," she remarks in a whisper-like tone.

Elijah speaks up, "The boat won't be on hand tomorrow, Chloe." His heavy tone carries the weight of his words.

"Why is that?" Chloe questions startled.

"Elroy and I need to do more scoutin' around, that's why," he says with a scorning face.

"There's been word of a fellah snooping nearby, so we thought it might be best to check it out," Uncle Elroy explains casually. His features are marred with scars. Rough and scraggly would pretty much fit the description of him. Not only does his voice have the same tenor as Elijah, but they have exactly the same sly eyes. I get the sense they're inherently true brothers, but one has a lot more stories to tell. He steals a look my way and then goes on shoveling in another bite of food.

"If you and Jess decide to go out after dinner. I'd advise to keep it short," Elijah grumbles pointing toward Chloe. She bobs her head up and down as she munches on boar and bread crust. Watching her eat is a show on its own. Crumbs sprinkle around her lips as she gives me a simple smile. The sound of a chair screeches back as Catherine rises, she begins gathering up empty plates. She stops beside me and says, "Grandmother Greta made a buttermilk pie, would you like some, David?"

I finish off the last morsel of meat on my plate, wipe my mouth with a napkin and reply, "Yeah, sure." She beams like I just made her night and walks toward the kitchen.

Silas yells out showcasing a lopsided grin, "I don't get any buttermilk pie, Catherine?!" He quickly wipes his mouth off and jumps up from the table, Jess playfully snaps her napkin at him as he rushes by.

"You're too dumb to get any pie, Silas!" Jess chuckles.

He hollers back from the kitchen, "I'm not that stupid to pass up Grandmother's pie!"

Finn excuses himself and heads to the other room where Catherine and Silas are, dividing out slices of pie. Laughter and mirthful voices occasionally echo from the kitchen. Hannah gently eases against the table and asks Greta, "What did you put in the dessert tonight, Grandmother?"

Greta leans forward, veering around Uncle Elroy, and replies sweetly, "I don't know what you're talkin' about child."

Hannah's smile grows with humor. "What did you do? Mix in a little love potion for an added zest?"

Greta chuckles softly as she gathers up her own plate. "We sure do need somethin' around here." As she leaves she sends a wink my way.

Elijah scoots his chair back and grunts, "Don't you be givin' these kids ideas, Greta. It's all a bunch of crap." He lifts a grey eyebrow up and carries on with, "There's just two things in this family that are understood." He shakes a finger at what little audience he has left. "Protect the family and leave love at the backdoor because there's no sense in it."

Elroy suddenly withdraws from his seat, a dark sneering look flashes over his face. "I think we all got the protect the family part, *brother*. But I also believe you forgot somethin'."

Elijah daringly juts his bearded chin outward and glares over to Elroy. "And what might that be?" he draws slowly out. With each word it's apparent there's a hostile intent as if this weren't a trivial dispute between the two. As the brothers bore holes through each other the room becomes quiet. Even the lighthearted laughter that crowded and mixed in the kitchen just a few seconds ago is nothing but dead air.

Hannah stands and subtly clears her throat. "*Ahem.*"

Elroy drags his scathing eyes away from Elijah and voices gruffly, "Sorry, Hannah." His hands tightly grip the chair like he's ready to break it in two, but he sucks in a heavy, determined breath and controls his emotions. Steadily, he finds her eyes again and says, "Maybe I should go…"

A sense of sadness washes over her face as she wrings the napkin in her hands. "Maybe," she replies and tries to offer him a light smile. In that small amount of time, the little interaction between Hannah and Elroy

I could already tell he was more of a father to her than her own. She was able to quiet the storm brewing inside him and he regarded her with respect.

Elroy lowers his head and then peers over to me. "David," he impassively says with a nod and starts walking toward the front door.

I raise my head up more and comment, "It was nice meeting you."

"Same," he replies and closes the door.

Chapter Fifteen

After dessert, Finn, and Silas venture outside with Jess and Chloe. Catherine and Grandmother Greta are tidying things up as I help Hannah with the dishes. I lean along the counter while Hannah rolls her sleeves up. A sink full of bubbles float gently around as she suds down a plate. I catch her sidelong glance toward me when she says, "Don't tell me, David. You're going to just stand there while I do the dishes?"

I lift my hands up and retort playfully, "What? You want me to leave?"

She scoffs, "No." And reaches for a clean dishtowel and tosses it to me. "You're going to help."

I slowly unbutton the cuff of my sleeve and push it up. "All you had to do was say the word."

She dunks a glass beneath the water, scrubbing with a sponge. And I watch how she moves, the way her hair falls against her cheek, the way she bites on her lip nervously. I'm sensing her guard slipping as she quietly laughs. "What?"

"Am I making you nervous?" I ask.

A blush rushes to her face. "No."

"You sure?" I question as our arms touch.

"Yes, I'm sure," she remarks rinsing off the glass and hands it to me. Her fingers barely graze mine and sends a quick look. As fleeting as her look was, I could feel a wave of heat flow through me. Even my own element can't control itself. I take another glass from her, but this time she makes sure our skin doesn't touch.

"I'm surprised by you," she openly admits keeping her focus on the dishes.

"I'm almost afraid to ask why," I reply and perch a dry glass on the counter.

"A man like you doing the dishes *and* he's not burning down someone's spellbound door."

"I'm sorry about that."

"Don't be. It was just a door, right?" she questions with a flippant tone.

I set another dry dish down. "Wait… what do you mean a *man* like me?"

She tries to hide her smile. "Let's just say you don't look like the type that does this?" She motions at the soapy sink filled with dinnerware. I run my thumb along the edge of my mouth and wonder what type of man she thinks I am, other than a spell-breaker.

"I can't really tell you about other men, but there's one thing I can tell you about me."

She stops mid-scrub and asks, "What's that?"

I nudge her arm and point at the cups and dishes sitting in the drainer. Every pot, pan, glass, and silverware are completely dry. I utilized my fire. I straighten my shirt and send her a flirty grin. "You wanna switch places and let me wash?"

She laughs. "You think you're something, don't you?"

I laugh at her comment in stride and state, "I don't know about something, but I know I'd be nothing without you." As the moment hits me, I grasp her chin and read her eyes as I mouth my words. *"I'm sorry. I... I didn't plan on saying that. It just came out, Hannah."*

She immediately inhales a breath and I know my words catch her off-guard just as much as it did me. I don't know what I was thinking, but I don't let go of her and try to decipher her expression. I watch carefully as she licks her lips and how her light-colored blues race over my face. She blinks a time or two and then she whispers, "Do you mean what you just said?"

"Yeah."

"It's not just some line you say to all the girls?"

"No."

"You sure?"

"Yeah," I reply truthfully.

"That's good," she remarks.

"What? How I dry dishes or what I just said?"

She tips her head to one side and softly replies, *"Both."*

My thumb lightly traces along her chin as our eyes search each other. "You want me to put them away?"

"Put what away?"

"The dishes?"

I chuckle inside with how we're both riveted to the moment. "What are you?" I ask sounding more absorbed by the second.

She creases her brows in confusion. "I'm just me."

"You're more than that."

"Well, that's reassuring, but I hate to break it to you," she says.

"What?" Now, it's my turn to offer her a concerned look.

"The glasses won't fit in the silverware drawer, David." she teases and points over to where I'm hovering a glass.

"Right," I comment with a wink. "Just making sure you were paying attention."

"Oh, I'm paying close attention," she says softly.

"Then I bet you won't see this one coming." I taunt and lean in to kiss her and just before our lips touch, I catch Elijah standing in the doorway. The glass I have airborne suddenly crashes to the floor. Hannah jumps as her hands tightly grip my shirt, and I'm a hundred percent sure it pisses off Elijah even more.

"Hannah!" he yells out to her. His bitter scowl penetrates through me. "It's supposed to get cold tonight. I need you to help stack the wood on the porch."

She moves away from me and an impenetrable shield slams dead in my face. It's like her emotions were instantly erased and she waltzes out of the backdoor with her father. Not a farewell glance or a toodle-oo as she leaves. I drag my hand through my hair and pace back and forth. *What the—?* Does she not feel the same way I do? Am I the only one that felt the burning chemistry orbiting around us? Am I just imagining this nerve-racking feeling? I work my jaw and force my hand outward. The broken glass clumps and melts together and I mentally drag it over to the trash. I drop to my knees and make sure there are no fragments left.

"Don't you worry about that, David," a gentle voice says behind me. I glance over my shoulder and see Grandmother Greta. "And don't you fret about them two either." She digs around a pantry and comes back with a broom and dustpan. "Here." She extends out the dustpan to me and smiles. "You just get whatever I sweep up."

"Okay," I quietly reply.

"You remind me of someone I knew when I was younger," she chuckles with a sparkle in her eyes.

"Oh, yeah?" I prop an elbow on my knee intrigued.

"He wasn't nothing like Elijah or my daughter, Catherine." She stops sweeping and stares off likes she's teleporting back to that time. And then she goes on, "He had a fire like you."

"Was he a fire element?" I curiously ask.

"No… but he sure knew what love was."

"He sounds like someone I'd liked to have met," I remark.

"Do you know what love is, David?" she questions holding the broom.

I drag in a serious breath and calmly reply, "I believe I do."

"Then you know, no love comes without sacrifice?"

I hold off my reply and think about Marc and Alyssa. There were moments in their relationship that tested every threshold of their love. I remember how Alyssa sacrificed herself to save some human bimbo named Kelly. And in return the demon Jinn took over Alyssa's body. Marc practically lost his ever-lovin' mind in that mayhem, but he figured out a way to get her back. And even in my own relationships, mainly with Naomi, I knew there would be a price to pay in the end.

"Yeah," I finally answer and chunk the last of the broken glass in the trash.

Greta ambles her way back to the pantry, placing the broom and dustpan away. "Hannah's a unique sort. She's never known anything else other than what her father has taught her. She's never traveled beyond these hills. And, I can say the same about Jessica and Chloe, but somethin' tells me you have your eyes set on Hannah more."

"Did you put something in that pie of yours, Grandmother Greta?" I joke crossing my arms over my chest.

She props a hand on her round hip and laughs. "Goodness gracious, child. What do you think I am?"

I raise my hands up. "Okay, okay…just thought I'd ask."

She wags a small finger toward me. "But I will tell you this…you could live a thousand lives in a thousand different ways, but you'll always be able to spot love. And I don't mean the hanky-panky adolescent love. I mean the mark of the crescent moon. It'll bleed red when bound to a lifemate. No one around here has the faintest notion of what I'm talkin' about because it's just nonsense to them. But if my witchy instincts are right about you, then you know what I mean."

I lean off the counter a bit. "Wait, are you telling me there's not a witch here that hasn't been bound by the mark?"

"Well, if there is, they're hiding it pretty well. After what happened to Elroy and Savannah it all came to a stop. And only one thing took precedence over the coven, and I'm here to tell you it wasn't love."

"That's why there was tension between Elijah and Elroy earlier?" I ask.

She nods pensively.

"And Savannah?"

"Sadly, honey, she's no longer with us," she replies.

"Then why doesn't he just leave this place?"

"I think he stays mainly for the girls. He's always been there and tried to do right by them."

"So, why are you telling me all this?" I ask helping her stack the plates in the cabinet.

She grins and I see every smile-line wrinkle. "I just thought you should know there's choices everyone here has made, some bad and some good. And if

Hannah fancies you like you do her, then she'll have to decide."

<hr>

After talking and helping Greta cleanup, I have a better grasp on Hannah's behavior with me, *or* at least I think I do. Eventually, I make my way out to the back porch and breathe in the cool, crisp air. I roll my sleeves down and button the cuffs. The lake is about fifty feet away. The water ripples with the reflection from the glistening stars above. It's quiet and reclusive and then I hear laughter from the cabin beside the lake. Lights glow softly through each window, and I recognize a dark figure striding up.

"Did you get stuffed or are you a glutton for punishment?" Silas bellows out. "Cus I know I sure could devour all of Grandma Greta's buttermilk pie."

I soften my glare and answer back, "No, I'm just taking in the night."

He halts his steps and looks up. "Yeah, it's somethin' out here. I don't know what it is, whether it's the lake or—"

"The girls," I chime in and jog down the steps.

He chuckles at my comment. "Yeah, it's probably the girls. So… are you goin' to be around for long?"

"I'm not sure."

"Must be nice to travel the world, see different places and all," he says shoving his hands inside his pockets. "What's it like?"

"Traveling?" I ask, glancing over to him.

"Yeah," he replies staring up at the sky.

"It's different. I mean every place has its distinctiveness. Always journeying from one place to another you never know what to expect sometimes."

Silas chuckles to himself. "Well, at least you don't have expectations riding your ass. You can come and go as you please."

"That's true."

He motions over his shoulder and says in a lower voice, "I've had my eye on someone here for the longest time, but as most know around these parts if you don't have the father's blessing then you're out of luck."

"How so?" I question.

Silas makes sure his back faces the main house. "Well…not many get to pick who they wanna be with. It's mostly up to the parents. This all probably sounds old school to you, I'm sure, but it's the way our coven works." He sends a quick smirk and rocks back on his heels like he's divulging a highly classified matter. "I brought somethin' to Elijah that I knew would be a surefire way he'd promise Hannah to me."

I snap my head in his direction and rumble out, "Hannah?"

"Yeah. See? I'm not as dumb as Chloe thinks I am." He laughs.

Countless questions start rolling through my mind. "What did you bring him?"

"A book. I know what you're thinkin', but it's no ordinary book though."

"It's not?" I ask casting my gaze out toward the water.

"No, this book of shadows has helped us for a few years now. I guess you could say it's pretty much assured our safety when the full moon hits." His proud grin spreads wider as he carries on, "And nothin' beats what I brought Elijah. I just hope Hannah sees it for what it is."

I glance over to him. "A token of your love?"

He laughs. "I guess you could call it that." I note him peering my way briefly and adds, "You know how women are, David, always tormenting us. I just decided to take fate into my own hands."

"What about Chloe? You two seemed pretty friendly at dinner?" I ask.

He shrugs and shakes his head. "Yeah, she's cute and all, but she's more like a little sister to me. Besides, Hannah's got the looks and she's quiet. I think she's smart enough to let a man do whatever was necessary to protect the coven."

"Sounds like you've got it all figured out," I remark.

He looks up, studying the stars, and lets out a gratified sigh, "*Yeah,* I think I've finally outdone myself."

I narrow my gaze and casually ask, "This book of shadows you gave to Elijah… what all did it contain?"

He quickly combs back his red hair before he looks over to me. "Sigils, different symbols and—"

"Hey, you two, what are you doing up here?" Chloe questions walking toward us. Her bouncy stride matches her lively expression. "I thought you were coming right back, Silas?" She switches her eyes away from him and smiles over to me. "C'mon, David. We're all just down there, see? It's not far." She aims at the cabin nestled along the lake.

Silas motions behind him and says, "I was going to grab some more pie, but I think David beat me to it."

"Who cares about pie when we're all having fun at my place," she laughs walking backward. "I swear you two are as slow as molasses in the dead of winter. C'mon!" She yanks on Silas' arm, and then mine, dragging us along. We follow a small rock path leading from the main house and right up to Chloe's cabin. "Bet you didn't think I had my own place, did you, David?"

"I really didn't put too much thought in it," I reply, keeping my tone from sounding offensive.

Chloe stops just a few feet away from the structured area in front of the cabin. "Just on the other side of the ridge over there is Jess' cabin. She didn't want to be too close to the water and she has a little more privacy, too. So, when my father decided to build these he made sure they were near the main house, but it also gave us our personal space."

I get the distinct impression she wants me to ask her something but the only thing that comes to mind is, "Is Hannah's place close by too?"

"Oh, well, of course, she has to be secluded. So much so, that father and Hannah did have a war of words over it, but finally, he built it just through the thicket of woods over there," she explains. She begins to show us the direction to the cabin when Jess pops her head out.

"What are you guys waiting on?!" Jess yells from the porch.

Out of the corner of my eye, I catch movement over by the dock. The feminine figure looks ethereal as her green dress flows with the nightly breeze. It's Hannah. She faces the unfading waters like she's searching for answers along the shimmering surface. The whole scene of her captivates me and I barely register Chloe calling out my name.

"David?"

"Yeah?"

"Are you coming?" Chloe asks.

"I might later. I'm going to check on something," I state quickly and stride out to the dock.

Chapter Sixteen

Hannah never startles as I approach her, and we stand in silence for a moment. "I thought I felt something witchy come this way," she finally says. A hushed smile hints at her lips.

"Thought you could use some company."

"Are you implying that I was lonely?" she questions looking over to me.

"No, but maybe I was," I comment trying to contain my chuckle.

"Don't tell me my sisters are not entertaining enough?"

I rub along my mouth and try my damndest not to smile. "No, they're, *um*, definitely entertaining."

"So, what's the problem?" she asks.

"I never said there was a problem. Just thought I'd keep a beautiful woman like yourself company."

That remark earns me a chuckle from her as she replies, "There goes another one of your lines, David."

Her fingers delicately thread through her hair, brushing it away from her face.

"So, is this how you spend your time other than working and reading books?"

"You make it sound so trivial."

"That's not what I meant."

Her expression softens as she glances at me. "I'm not trying to give you a hard time, David. It's just—"

"No, I think your whole goal in life is to plague me with your charm."

She smiles and retorts, "Charm?"

"See you have the killer looks and charm, and all I have is my witty wisecracks. We're destined to be together. Can't you see?"

"Well, it's not how my father sees it," she says softly and starts to walk away.

I tag along, internally thanking the Gods for every faint scent from her perfume. It's tranquilizing yet maddening. And maybe it's not entirely the scent of her. Maybe it's the way she easily tosses her silk-like hair to one side and cheats me that one more sensual glance. I smile inside and refrain myself.

"Are you making sure I get home safe?" she questions sending me a jeering look.

I shrug with my hands securely restrained in my pockets. "You never know what's lurking in these woods."

"Oh, now you have piqued my interest, David. Tell me what could possibly be in the woods?"

"Bugs, spiders, *wolves,*" I joke.

"I'm not afraid of any of that," she states and opens the door to her cabin. "I think this may surprise you, but the only thing that frightens me is you."

I give her a stumped look. "Me? Why is that?"

"I've seen guys like you, always saying the right things just to get the girl in bed." She slips inside the dark interior and lights an oil lantern.

I lean against the porch railing. "I take it you've already made an assumption of me without truly giving it a chance."

"It's either that, or you're just baiting me to find a book."

"Look, I'm—" I start to say when she opens the door farther and motions for me to come inside.

"Well…here's your chance. Take a look and see if I'm secretly hiding this mysterious book," she says graciously extending her arm out. I release the railing and step inside. The cabin is small, a wood-burning stove sits in one corner and a bed in the other. She has a desk facing the south window covered with various plants. The hallway light gives me enough view that I can tell there's no Hemlock or some other deadly herb stashed inside the clay pots. The place is spacious enough that she has another hall leading to a private bathroom and a linen closet. I find myself impressed with the engravings along her bookshelves in the foreroom. There's great detail in every etching. Each displays the phases of the moon. I glance back and ask, "Did your father make this?"

She nods leaning her back against the wall. I slip out a book and thumb through the pages. "Famous Affinities of History, huh?"

"If you're planning on borrowing it, then you better think again. It was written in 1909, the first edition. I'm still trying to locate the other volumes," she says evenly. "Besides, I don't believe you're the kinda guy that would read something like this anyway." She eases the book gently away and places it back in its rightful niche on the shelf.

"What else do you read?" I question sliding another book out.

She peeks around the bookshelf and gives me a candid look. "How to use plants for healing purposes, transformation mysteries, how to break curses. It's all up there."

"And the bookstore?"

"Ah… Now, that's where I keep all those demon books," she teases and walks over to a wooden nightstand. I glance over my shoulder and snap my fingers, lighting the lamp before she has a chance to. She stands with her back facing me. Softly she chuckles shaking her head. "I can see how that would be impressive."

"Are you saying you're impressed with me?" I ask placing the book back. Seizing the moment, I shift closer, diminishing the distance between us.

As she turns, she says, "Maybe a little."

"I'll take that as a, *yes,* then," I return. The intensity in the air increases, her eyes anxiously lock on mine and my mind starts playing out how she'll say, *kiss me, David.*

But, instead, she says, "What's it like?"

My dark brows furrow together in confusion. "What?"

"Your element? What's it like using it so freely?"

I see her eyes brighten with a youthful desire for knowledge. Her question is genuine and real, it's not a taunt or a jab. She sits on her bed quietly as if I'm going to give her a fairytale filled with the elements of fire, air, water, and earth and legends of the beyond.

I inhale, ease my hands in my back pockets and reply, "It's like second nature for me. I was taught at a place called the Arcane. Ever heard of it?" She slowly motions her head, *no,* and I go on explaining, "Well, there, you are taught how to work with your element. It's not about using it or possessing it. It's part of you, connected to you like how your fingers are connected to your hands."

"So, it's like an extension of yourself," she states.

"Precisely."

You may already know this, but our elements can feed off our own emotions and desires. Whether it's positive or negative. Good or bad, it still holds whatever emotions you have inside. Which is why at the Arcane they instruct you on how to have balance. It's crucial to have this balance; otherwise, you'll lose yourself and shit can hit the fan."

"I feel like our earth element has been just manipulated for our own survival. I know the elders say it wasn't always this way, but we have to accept it. Because change is good, but…" she voices and drifts off halting her next thought.

"But what?" I ask.

"But my father has changed somehow. I tried explaining this to Evan, but I think I made him more skeptical about me. I'm at a loss. I don't know how else to explain it." She sighs and drags her long blonde hair back. "I'm sorry. I don't have the book you're looking for, David."

I can tell this entire conversation bothers her. Her expression looks defeated and torn and it kills me inside to know that she feels like she's in this alone.

I kneel and cup her chin. "I know you don't have the book, Hannah. And don't worry about Evan. He's just jealous."

"Jealous of what?" she asks.

"Of what you and I have."

I watch as she smiles. "And what do you think we have, David?"

"This…" I move up and touch her tender lips with mine, and this time, I'm able to feel her give in. Our kiss starts off slow and unrushed but the more our mouths connect a fire blazes within. Passion and heat rises, and I grip her hair pulling her closer to me. Everything around me melts away and all I want is more of her. More of the insatiable urge and more of the compelling need to be with her. She tilts her head to the side allowing the perfect position to drive the kiss in deeper. I try to keep my fire at bay, I don't want to incinerate her room. We ascend together without breaking the kiss. Hungrily, she runs her fingers through my hair as we let go of all self-restraint.

And then there's an incessant, sudden knocking at her door. "Hannah? Are you okay? Hannah?" Silas' grating voice beckons.

Hannah pulls back, our foreheads softly touch as she whispers, "I have to answer him."

"Fuck him," I whisper back. Our breathing mirrors the mood of the room, heated and fierce. Our passion lingers firmly like an imprint left in a snowfield. "Let me get the door."

Her eyes focus on me as she smirks. "I can handle it."

"You sure?"

"Yeah, I'm sure," she confirms and breaks away from me. I drag my hands through my hair impatiently and sit on her bed.

A few seconds later I hear the door open. "Hey," Silas greets.

"Hey," Hannah replies.

"You okay?" he asks sounding troubled.

"Yes, I'm fine. Just doing some reading before bed."

"I just wanted to know everything was good, cus, I hadn't seen you since the celebration. I knew you… *we* took the elixir your father had made. I figured we'd be all right, but I thought it might be best to check in on ya anyway. So…you're okay?"

"Yeah, I'm fine."

"Well, I'm glad the Nakoa didn't capture you. They're gettin' pretty good at gettin' our kind nowadays."

"No, I wasn't captured as you can see."

"Yeah, I can see that." He lightly chuckles and then subtly adds, "You know…you looked really nice tonight."

"Thanks."

"I guess that guy, David, wandered off in the woods. His bike is still here, you think he's okay?"

"Yeah, I'm sure he's fine. I wouldn't worry too much about it, Silas."

I can hear Silas' hand grip the door as Hannah tries to keep it partially open. My fire urges to jump at any chance to torch the very spot he stands. I grind my teeth and ease back the raging impulse.

"You want me to keep you company before you go to sleep?"

"No, I think I'm good. I'm just going to call it a night. Okay, Silas?"

The boards on the porch creak and adjust as Silas moves. "Well… all right then. I'll see you maybe tomorrow?"

"I have to go in for work, so maybe later. Night, Silas."

"Night, Hannah," Silas replies as he loiters by the door.

Hannah waits a beat and finally closes it.

She enters the room while I lie back on her bed. With my arms crossed behind my head I ask, "I take it you don't like redheads?"

"No. I don't like egotistical males that think they're smarter than you," she sasses back.

"Point taken," I calmly reply. "So.. what are the Nakoa?"

"Not a what, but who…" she states and sits next to me. "Leah Nakoa comes from a long lineage. She's a member of one of three tribes that are known by many names. Savageness and bloodshed is one way to describe her kind and that's putting it mildly. If you remember the Lover's Leap story, then I can assure you they have formulated their own reason to hunt. And they hunt with skill and agility like none of us have ever seen. You would think they were born with our traits, but either way, no matter how the story goes, a descendant of her family was bewitched. There was no room for talking or reasoning with them. It was like a prickly thorn in their side that festered and ever since then it's been Wolfenstein vs Nakoa. And let's just say, we're a dying breed and you can thank the Nakoa for that."

"Well, I can take care of that for you," I remark.

"You think it's that easy?"

"I never said it would be easy, Hannah."

She drops her tan toe-ringed sandals to the floor and curls her legs beneath herself and states, "I see their side though, David. Their livelihood was once taken from them. Over a hundred years ago they had fought hard to maintain their own sacredness and what they believed the Gods had provided them. And it was all taken from them. So, if you see it from the opposite perspective— it's a sense of justice. It has always been their way of life. We're no different."

"You say that like you understand their anguish," I remark.

"How would you feel if someone came in and took *everything* you valued and wiped it all away?"

"I'd set the world on fire," I answer honestly.

"Exactly," she replies.

I close my eyes and listen to her explanations of how she sees the reasons for the Nakoa and I fall for her even more. She's not stuck on retribution or loathing. She's just trying to survive in the chaos that dwells in Mistcove.

I motion for her to come closer. "Come here."

She slowly moves toward me. "Don't you see? This isn't necessarily about—"

I grip her face and kiss her mid-sentence. Golden tresses fall softly against my face as she gains leverage over me. This kiss comes more naturally. More unbreakable like we have all the time in the world to enjoy this moment. With my other hand, I follow the long soft curls down to her neck and start releasing one button at a time. Exposing the thin fabric beneath, I caress her breast. She moans lightly against my mouth and moves away. "Here, let me help you," she says in a breathy voice. I watch as she slips the dress up and over her head letting golden ringlets tumble downward. She glides a finger along the edge of her bra and unclasps it from behind. Her breasts are fully uncovered as she sits on me.

"Did you think I was going to take too long unbuttoning your dress?" I ask dragging my eyes away from her perky, pink nipples.

"Maybe," she replies.

I sit up gripping her sides. "You know how I take your *maybes?* They're as good as a *yes* to me."

She smiles. "Then *maybe* I want you to touch me here…" She takes my hand and guides it to her other breast. Gently, I squeeze and rub my thumb along her silklike skin. Her head leans back as she closes her eyes. A dreamy sigh escapes her as I run my hands over her perfect body. I lower my wandering fingers and lay her beneath me. Her hair fans out across the pillow and all I can think about is how she resembles a goddess in the dimly lit night.

I unbutton my shirt, toss it to the floor and I begin kissing her neck. I touch my lips along her delicate collarbone and then I cup her breast. Slowly, I twirl my tongue around each nipple and trek all the way down to her stomach just above her navel. Her hands feverishly thread through my hair as I look up to her. As if she knows my next quest she asks, "Am I going to see fireworks, David?"

"Maybe."

"Then, your *maybe* is as good as a *yes* to me."

She places her head back down on the pillow and I slide off her panties with the crook of my finger. My hands travel a heated trail along her long, slender legs. A fire churns inside like a beast waiting to be unleashed, but I reign it in and spread her legs. My mouth consumes her while I stroke and lick. Her body arches and grinds against me as she lustfully groans. I'm driven with desire and a burning need to please her in every way possible. Her legs begin to tremble, her breathing amplifies, and I can feel the second her climax quickly mounts. One more stroke from my tongue and she quivers beneath my wet lips.

"David…" she calls out, her tone impatient and sensual. With lightning-like speed, I slide my boots off and then my jeans and move above her.

Making sure we're protected I glance down at her and ask, "Are you taking—"

"Yes," she replies knowing exactly what I am asking without having to go into detail. I recline back and grip her hips and thrust inside. Every part of me wants to explode. She has this insane ability to taunt my fire and tease me in the same breath but subdues it all with just a simple touch. I rock my hips building a steady rhythm and cradle my body closer. I search her face because something starts to happen as our eyes lock. Her moans turn into a sharp, unsteady breath. A white-hot glow faintly shimmers along her bare skin as my element binds to hers. My own flesh begins to pulsate as our magick connects. My veins contort and twist making it look like vines of fire. All along my arms, my chest and down my back I'm completely covered.

I know what this means, it's the sign of a lifemate because this has never happened with any other woman before. I also know there's a monumental step that needs to be taken.

"Hannah? Do you want this?" I ask with a serious tone.

"Do you?"

"Of course, I do," I reach up and brush aside a curl from her face. "Okay," I whisper and scan around the room.

"What is it, David?"

"Where's your athame blade?"

"It's over there by the window. I was going to charge it tomorrow in the sunlight."

I don't want to move from her, so I try to visualize the blade and summon it to me. It takes a second, but it quickly soars through the air and I grip the handle in my hand. I lean down and kiss her lips. "You sure about this?"

Her fingertips gently trace my jaw and down my neck. In-between kisses she whispers, "Yes."

I take one of her hands away and drag the blade along her palm. She flinches and looks at me with the same innocent look she gave me earlier. "Now, there's no going back once I cast the spell."

"You make this sound like it could have adverse consequences," she returns.

"It could. So…you still want to do this?"

She glances at her hand like she's seriously reflecting on the outcome, but then she says, "Is it true what they say…lifemates are bound forever?"

"They are bound, but only in death will this spell break. I will protect you with my life just as you would for me. I'll know if you need me and I will cherish you just as a true lover should."

She offers her hand to me and I know she's ready. I begin casting the spell, kissing her open palm gently, and recite the words, "By the blood of my blood, I bind you to me. For all of time, and through eternity, fire begets earth within our runes. May our bodies dance by the powers of the moon. Throughout all of time as one we'll be, by the blood of our blood. So, mote it be."

I turn the blade from her hand and cut along my own palm. She kisses my hand where I made the mark and repeats the words. Even with the small droplets of blood, it's enough to fulfill the spell. She's mine and I am hers. I place the athame on the nightstand and set in motion what we had started. The concept hits me as I run my gaze over her body, *she's bound to me*. The possessive thought makes my hands tighten, and right along with that thought, my fire provokes my movements. I kiss her like I'm dying to taste more of her. I'm overwhelmed with the sweet vanilla scent of her hair and the softness of her skin. I'm taking it all in as the spell embeds in my core and I memorize every single inch of her. I listen to the sounds she makes each time I move and thrust. I watch how her full, beautiful lips part as a moan grinds out again. And just on the brink of our first surge together I hear her faintly mutter, "*Oh, David*…this is more than I could've ever imagined."

Just my name rushing from her mouth sends me over the edge.

It's a quarter past midnight, Hannah's resting beside me. Her fingertips move smoothly over my chest. "David?" she asks quietly.

"Yes?"

"Is this real?"

I roll on to my side and reply. "Go look in the mirror at the crescent mark and then come back and tell if it's real or not."

Her eyes fall on my left upper arm as she scoots up. She gently touches the same mark on me and asks, "Blood bound?"

I nod. "I'm guessing you've read about it, otherwise, you wouldn't have asked about it before."

"I have, it's just strange to experience this because our coven doesn't allow it. It's forbidden in my father's eyes."

"Why?"

She sends me a distressing look. "My father believes if you follow the path of the divine then you will be cleansed of all the past sins. The curse will one day be lifted, and our elements will be fully recovered. So, that's why *they* select a pairing."

"Has Silas been chosen for you?" I ask.

"I've never agreed to it. I've tried to keep my distance from him. I practically begged my father to pick someone else as queen for the Beltane. But he wouldn't listen, and with the way the elders see it, if you're stronger, faster, and have the ability to move through the woods then there are no questions to be asked. You will be chosen. It's survival of the fittest."

"So, the night I found you…" I trace my fingers over the slight scar on her side. "What happened?"

She moves her body closer to me and says, "I only remember bits and pieces. I was supposed to divert the Nakoa's group and lead them to the other side of the woods. But they had already split up and then…"

"You were hit."

"And you saved me," she whispers against my chest.

"The elixir? Was it in the chalices the night of the celebration?"

"Yeah, my father always mixes different tinctures for each Sabbat, and each season the drinks become more potent and more nauseating." She lightly chuckles, "It's so bad that Chloe and Jess can barely keep it down. But he insists we drink it because it has healing properties." She takes my two fingers and slides them over the small, raised flesh on her side and says, "It does, otherwise, I would be in a lot worse shape than I am now."

I move my hand lower and feel the curve of her hip, and then slowly drag my hand around, touching the imprint on her lower back. Heat courses through the crescent shaped mark. I know I have to protect her because her father sounds like an occult fanatic. He's slipping the Demon's blood in their drinks. I grind my teeth thinking about how Silas gave the book of shadows to Elijah, and Hannah has no clue what they're scheming. Each gnawing feeling rolls into the next, and

I know Elijah has gone far beyond scratching the surface of owning the book, he's sacrificing too.

"David?"

"Yeah?"

"What are you thinking?"

I redirect my gaze and tuck a wisp of hair behind her ear. "How gorgeous you are."

"Hmm," she retorts and moves to her back.

"What's the *hmm* for?"

"It's not the look you had."

"It's not?" I question.

"No."

"Okay, what kinda look was it then?"

"Like you were having murderous thoughts."

I had no idea I was exhibiting my internal feelings. "Actually, I was thinking about Silas…you, and what would happen if he ever decides to touch you."

"That's not going to happen," she replies with confidence.

I lean over on my elbow. "I know how guys are, Hannah, when they're dead-set on a girl."

"You say this like you've experienced it before." She grins lifting a brow.

"Maybe…"

"Really? I never saw you as the jealous type. I mean with your witty comebacks and all. I thought you'd have women chasing you night and day."

"Well, now there's only one woman I want," I reply and crush my lips to hers ceasing her next words.

After a few moments kissing I note her breathing slows, her body stills, and I watch over her as she falls asleep. I decide it's probably best to leave before her sisters start banging on her door, or worse, her *father*. I slide out of bed, quietly get dressed, and head out.

Chapter Seventeen

I hike up the road and spot Uncle Elroy sitting outside on his cabin porch. He's bent over puffing on a cigarette in a creaky, old rocking chair. "Hey, boy," he hollers.

I stop my stride and take a quick look around. "Yeah?"

"Nice night out, don't ya think?"

Feeling more alive than I ever have, I steal a moment and stare up at the beautiful stars. A light breeze carries the scent from a firepit burning off to one side. Insects chirp beside the lake, and a lone owl hoots from a tree above. "Really nice," I reply and make my way toward the porch.

He drags an empty chair up and offers it to me. "Why don't you sit a spell," he chuckles at his own pun and slicks back his greasy, black hair. The embers from his cigarette glow brightly as he takes in a drag. "Not a lot of nights like these, you know?" he questions, skimming a look my way. I'm not sure if he saw me leaving Hannah's cabin, or not, but I get the undertone from his gravelly voice that he suspects something.

I relax and grip the arms of the chair and let out a sigh. "Nope, I guess not."

"You know, it's nights like these that make me realize how fucked up this coven is."

I ease back in the chair and easily reply, "I can't really say, Elroy."

He aims his fingers with the lit cig toward me and narrows his surly eyes. "Don't you tell me, boy, you don't see it."

He's got my full attention, and I lean over on my knees and stare at him. "See what?"

"*Shit*," he draws out slowly. Maybe I focus too long on the scars across his face or the one that cuts deep through his jawbone. He snaps his head in my direction and clenches his teeth. "You think I got these scars for some kinda pride thing? Virtuous battle wounds?" He laughs to himself and takes a swig from whatever he's drinking. "They ain't pretty, I'll tell you that much." He slumps back in the old chair and huffs out a heavy sigh. "You know, boy, there comes a time when someone has to draw a line and they have to decide." He motions his hand still cradling the cigarette and says, "Family, blood, or love." He chuckles softly like it's all a joke to him.

I look away and remark, "I didn't come here for love."

Elroy grunts without an inkling of humor. "No one beats the bushes to be bound." He sends me a squinty-eyed look. "Yeah, I know how it goes. No one figures they'll be smitten by that one girl, but when it happens there's nothin' like it." He spins his fingers making the smoke fan out. "A long time ago, I was a lot like you. Clouded by all the hype, but you got another thing comin' if you think it's all sunshine and fuckin' lollipops."

I meet his eyes. "I never said it was."

"You say that now, but just a word of warnin', her father has already crossed that line, and this blood may just be thicker than water in that aspect." His tobacco dies out.

"Here, let me help," I approach, ready to provoke my flames.

He waves me off. "Naw, I got it." He taps the end of the roll and stirs a familiar light. "Elements like us tend to be less common in these parts, but just so you know, lifemates hold more advantages than any other muscle in this shithole."

"Lifemates and being bound, you make this sound like—"

"Like it's hot-water? Damn straight its fuckin' hot-water." He pokes at his chest. "I should know. I've lost the one thing that truly mattered to me." Whether he intended it to appear or not, the silhouette of a woman forms in the puff he expels. "I think back to those times and wonder what I could've done differently."

The sounds of nature surround us, and I let the moment settle in silence. No one described Elroy's past to me, but I come to grips with the fact that he influences the element of fire. He's loved and lost a lifemate. The turmoil twisting in him, still to this day, lashes at him, and every scar evokes the memories of her.

"I guess what I'm tryin' to say, boy, is just because you've got the girl doesn't mean you're over the bloodshed. You just keep your head above water, know what I'm sayin'?"

I nod my head soaking up his words, and then I lift myself from the chair. Before I walk off the porch, I ask over my shoulder, "This is Demon's blood you're telling me about?" Gradually, I look over to him. The dark circles beneath his eyes show he's tired and dejected, but it also shows he's seen things he wishes he hadn't. He takes another swig from a bottle sitting next to him and props a scrawny elbow on his knee.

"Demon's blood, family blood, it doesn't make a damn difference anymore," he grumbles and flicks the cigarette across the porch. "You can thank Elijah for that, him and that occult lovin' Brotherhood."

"The Brotherhood of the Raven?"

"Call it what you want, rain or shine you're still standin' in the same fuckin' calamity."

I turn away and slide my hands inside the front pockets of my jeans. "Thanks for the talk, Elroy," I say as my boots hit the last step.

Halfway around the porch, I hear him mutter, "Don't make the same mistakes I did, David."

Chapter Eighteen

I ride my bike back into town. The sun still hasn't revealed its rays of light. Vague and murky shadows cling to the streets like a sentimental lover. I dwell in the moments with Hannah and every detail from Grandmother Greta to Elroy. I've never let my emotions cloud my mission in destroying the Brotherhood. Now, I'm just trying to grasp the enormity of it all. The whereabouts of the book are somewhat clearer. The exact location I'm still learning, but the why and how it's fallen into the Wolfenstein territory I understand better. Love, or the illusion of love, can make a man do just about anything.

My kickstand scrapes against the pavement as I park my bike. Evan's most likely going to give me some kind of in-depth debriefing when I enter the hotel room. As soon as I drop my keys on the desk beside the door I realize I've forgotten my jacket at her parent's house. This entire time I never thought twice about it and it's one of my favorite jackets. The Gods must have wiped my memory clean the moment I set eyes on Hannah.

"Hey," I greet Evan walking into the room.

He peeks up from the laptop sitting in front of him. "So how did everything go?"

"Pretty good. I know who has the book," I announce.

He closes the laptop and eyes me like I'm kidding around. I take a seat across from him and start untying my boots.

"Let me guess…Hannah?" Evan questions.

"Nope."

"One of her sisters?"

"Nope," I calmly remark and throw the boots to the side. "Her father, Elijah."

"I wonder how he got the book?"

I lean over on my knees and reply, "You're not going to believe this, but a guy named Silas brought the book to Hannah's father. A bargaining chip to get something in return."

"And what did he want in return?"

"Hannah," I state knowing this all sounds twisted and kinda disturbing.

"Okay… so does this Silas guy know the book summons a demon?"

"I don't think he really cares what it's used for, Ev. He wanted something to impress Elijah."

Evan moves so fast it takes me a second to realize he's not sitting on the bed. "We have to get the book back, David," he sternly says yanking his trench coat on.

"Whoa, Ev. Slow your roll there, we can't just go up to Hannah's parents' house, knock on the door and say, '*Can I have that book? You know, the one that conjures up a demon?*'"

Evan releases the doorknob. "You're right." He flicks his long coat tail back and places his hands on his hips while pacing. "Do you know exactly where in the house it's located?"

"No, I just know the book was given to Elijah."

"Maybe Hannah or one of her sisters know where it is," Evan remarks.

"The girls know nothing about the book or what it can do, thankfully."

"You sure?" he asks and stops his pacing.

"I'm positive, Ev. I think you have to understand something about this family. They're like simple countrified witches and their beliefs are way different than ours. They don't believe in lifemates, their powers are restricted because of the curse, and the father thinks if he can control things, then he's walking some righteous path. I don't think they truly know what they have. I mean, fuck, Silas thinks the book is a token of his love."

"Then it shouldn't be too hard to get the book from them," Evan says and starts whipping out all kinds of maps. He motions for me to come closer to the desk. "I found out from Leah and Malcolm there are secret paths and roads that lead out of town. She said some can take you underground. So, I started outlining the scope of things, you know, around the area and look…" He takes his finger and slowly drags it along a road, but the path abruptly stops. "Do you know where this would have led if it were shown on the map?"

"No."

"The Willowshire building. The reason it doesn't show is because it's belowground. The only way Leah and I got to it, that one day she showed me, was hiking through the woods. So, maybe there's a different way to the Wolfenstein's house than the obvious."

"Yeah, okay, but I think there's something to consider before we search and destroy," I state and walk away.

"Okay, what's there to consider?"

"Hannah. We're crescent bound, and it's not about just getting the book any more—"

"You have to protect your lifemate. I can understand that," Evan says evenly. He doesn't express the words like he's being patronizing nor perturbed. He's says it like he knew something changed, and it has— she's part of the equation now, and we have to take extra precautions with her in mind.

I hear him folding up the maps as he clears his throat. "I knew you were bound to her, because I could smell her perfume the second you walked in. And just so you know, David, I'm kinda relieved you've found your mate. Not many of us do in this life, so…"

"So, now you can stop being jealous?" I laugh.

"Who says I was ever jealous? Besides, we've got other matters to attend to," he remarks and throws me the keys to my bike. "Go grab us some breakfast, it's going to be a long day ahead."

Before I start to stride out, I slide my boots back on. "Oh, wait, I have a serious question to ask…Do you want the sprinkle of farm fresh blueberries on the side of your pancakes or on top? And is it two thin strips of bacon or three?"

As I close the door behind me, I hear something heavy hit. Whatever he tossed was hard enough to make the handle shake in my hand. I chuckle inside and leave the hotel.

Chapter Nineteen

It takes me nearly all damn day to talk Evan into my plan. The way I see it, the chances of Hannah finding the book are higher than Evan and me snooping around. He also knows that the longer the book is used the more destructive it can become. And I'm not talking about the ones using it. In order to use the book, you have to have a living breathing body to support the possession for the demon embodiment. Of course, there's the sigils and a witch's circle to contain all this, but the key thing is a sacrifice has to be made to obtain the demon's blood.

I don't know if Elijah has decided to manipulate human tourists, the Nakoa, or whom for this, but I'd hate to think he would have used someone like Elroy's lifemate. It sickens me to even think that, but with how Elijah and Elroy held so much loathing toward each other, I get something really bad went down. The bottom line is— lives are at stake and we have to stop it.

Hannah's supposed to be off work in about five minutes, and I decide to chill out in front of The

Witchery. With my back against the wall, one knee bent, I wait for her to come out. Laughter trills out as the door opens, and the first thing I see is Silas' fiery red hair and then Hannah walking beside him. My blood boils and I clench my teeth trying to keep my control. Being bound to someone jumps things to the next level. I never quite understood why Marc acted so fucking possessive over Alyssa, but now I know why.

"Oh. Hey, there, David," Silas greets me wearing a cheeky smile.

"Hey," I grind out, plastering a bogus grin.

Hannah grazes her hand gently across my arm like she's soothing a feral animal. "David…Silas was just asking to go hang out at the apple orchard."

Silas intervenes nervously, "Well, ah…I was meaning, Hannah—"

"Yeah, sure! I don't think I've ever been to an apple orchard before," I reply holding an eager tone.

Silas scratches the back of his head and I watch as he tries to think of a way to exclude me from the scenario he's played out. "Ya know, I completely forgot I had somethin' to do…" he says backing away. "But… maybe we can…"

"Hang out another time?" I ask.

"Yeah." He darts a fleeting look toward Hannah and then my way. Before I know it he's jogging off and out of our sight.

"Well, I guess Silas didn't want me to tag along, and here I thought we'd make great buddies. We'd have a lot to talk about," I wisecrack.

"You are terrible. You know that, right?" Hannah sasses, shaking her head.

I catch her hand and pull her closer. "I don't recall those words coming from you last night."

She blushes, takes a quick glimpse around making sure no one's watching, and softly says, "Of course, I didn't say that last night because it was amazing."

"Just amazing?" I tease.

She tugs on my hand and smiles that stunning smile of hers. "Okay, mind-blowing. Is that better?"

I lean off the wall and follow her down the sidewalk. "I think I can live with that. Mind-blowing, huh?"

She laughs and I'm captivated by her beauty. The way the sun strikes every feature of her face it would make you think she's immortal.

"Coming?"

"Where are we heading?" I ask.

"To the orchard."

"Okay…"

She peeks over her shoulder at me. "I thought you said you'd never been to an apple orchard before?"

"I haven't, I don't think…*maybe*—"

"It's okay either way. I just thought it would give us some alone time."

"All right. Sounds good to me," I promptly reply.

———

I get the perception mostly everyone around here walks. I've seen several parked cars along the streets, but it's mainly the travelers passing through or staying a few nights. Hannah swiftly cuts through different side streets and up a small path. The gift shops become less and less as we proceed through wooded land. Hannah grips the lower part of her floral-patterned dress and starts to hop over a fallen branch, but I seize the moment and take her in my arms. "Oh! David!" she exclaims in surprise. "What are you doing?"

Cradling her close to me, I grin. "Saving you, once again from these treacherous woods."

She laughs. "You know what I think?"

"What's that?"

"You're going down the wrong path."

I halt my steps, there were two separate deer trails and I had taken the one on the left. "Okay, easy fix." I turn around and head in the right direction.

"I was wondering if I would see you again after last night," she says softly.

I scrunch my brows together puzzled. "What? Why would you think that after what I told you? We're bound. Nothing could ever take me away from you."

"But aren't you and Evan going to leave once you find the book you're looking for?"

"I'm not leaving here without you," I reply.

"Maybe we haven't thought this through, David. If my father finds out about us I don't know what he'll do. And the elixir he makes helps when we change…"

I let her slide out of my arms so she can stand. The orchard stretches out as far as the eye can see. White blooming trees form perfect rows, one after the next, and it feels magical with the pale glow sparkling from them. A strong fragrant scent hovers through the air like an enchantress casting a forbidden spell.

"What is this place?" I ask sounding dazed.

"The orchard."

I walk forward and gently touch a leaf. It feels real, but as I move my fingers away the soft, white-orange glow stays with me. Rubbing my fingertips, I can feel it absorb through my skin. I turn to Hannah. "Is this your element?"

"No, it's *our* element. This is what my family produces together. There's no way I could ever do *this* by myself."

"Who told you that?" I ask.

"My father. He says our powers are stronger when we're together. This is our livelihood, we can offer an abundance of food for this area, plus, it establishes a sense of natural rights to the land. But the Nakoa refused any type of agreement with him."

"Hannah? Have you tried using your element since last night?"

She waits a beat before she answers, "No. Why?"

I take her by the hand. "Come here, I wanna try something."

We walk toward a section which is open and flat, I kneel, and she follows my movement. "Remember what I said about lifemates? There's a connection between us, and I don't just mean the physical intensity of it. Our elements can develop more, making *us* stronger. Making *you* stronger in your own unique way. So… here's what I want you to do." I place her hand on the ground and let go of her. "Now, close your eyes and call your element. Try to visualize what you want to grow there. Okay?"

She tucks her legs underneath herself and closes her eyes. I can tell she's concentrating with the way she creases her brows. I have no idea if this will work because if it's true about the curse it may block out our bond. Her fingers desperately grasp at the earth as if she's trying to force something to sprout up. I patiently wait, but after a few seconds pass, I whisper, "Remember, you don't control the element, you work with it."

I rest my arm over one knee and wait another second or two, and then her hand starts to shake. Vines push through the ground and wrap around her hand, slowly a twig slithers in between her fingers. It grows and rises higher and the full form of it begins to manifest. A sapling. It's no taller than a chunk of firewood. She peeks one eye open and lets out an exasperated sigh. "I can't do this, David. Not without the others. I told you, we have *always*—"

"Yes, you can, Hannah. You're not alone," I voice tenderly.

"But…"

I rest my hand on hers and encourage her, "Try it again, but this time I want you to think bigger. See that strip of trees over there?"

She swallows nervously. "Yes."

"Think of how you would create it. Think of all the books you've read and how each story unfolded in your mind. Let your imagination go."

She exhales another frustrated sigh. Gradually, she closes her eyes again, and this time she doesn't grip the earth like she's manhandling it. I keep my hand on hers and add a little spark to the flames, so to speak, letting her know I'm here and guiding her along. A moment slips by and then the soil moves beneath our hands. The vines that wrapped around her hand creep back into the ground and I can feel a vibration run along her skin. I release my hand from her and quietly watch as the trees across from us tremble. Ivylike vines wind and twist, embracing each tree, every branch spreads outward with blossoming flowers. Different rich shades of pinks, blues, violets, and whites embellish everything. The grass below looks greener, more vivid, and before I know it I'm looking at an enchanted forest. And it's breathtaking.

I hear a gasp from Hannah as she opens her eyes. "David?"

"Yeah?"

"We did it..." she whispers mystified.

"No, you did it," I remark, watching her stunned expression.

"*Wha—No*, we did it together," she says glancing down. She quickly realizes I had moved my hand away. We mirror each other standing up, her smile is just as big as mine. She locks her arms fiercely around my neck. "Oh, my gosh! David, I can't believe this! I just can't! I'm so happy I could kiss you."

"Then what are you waiting for? More flowers to bloom?" I taunt grinning. Her lips crush against mine, and I can still feel the energy coursing through her. I tilt my head, deepening the kiss and savoring the taste of her. Her hands anxiously grip my hair. Mine are so entangled in hers that I don't even care if we walk back out of here looking like savages from another world. I walk her backward with me and into the flowery paradise she created. "What are you doing?" she questions brushing her mouth along mine.

"You don't think I'm going to let this moment go to waste, do you?"

Her lips barely a breath away, she whispers, "Then lead me with your fire and I will follow."

"Oh, yeah?" I ask grazing my mouth along hers. "You sure you're ready for this?"

"Yeah, I'm sure."

I release her hair and allow my flames to swirl down my arms. In one sweep I grasp her waist, red hot coils fan outward and then I hear her cry out. "Ouch!"

My fire dies out in an instant. "What? Are you okay?" I immediately ask.

She laughs. "I was just teasing you."

I sweep her off her feet and carry her deeper into the woods. "Now, you're going to get it. You know that, right?"

"Am I? Flames and all, huh?"

Karli Rush

"Flames and all, baby," I retort.

Chapter Twenty

Hannah and I get dressed and try to look somewhat normal. Her tangled hair still has leaves and twigs in it and I quickly realize I have my t-shirt on inside out.

"I'm glad you didn't catch the woods on fire," she admits combing her fingers through her hair.

"Yeah, that probably would've raised an alarm." I drop her a quick wink and ask a question that's been burning in my mind, "What do you think your family would do if they knew about us?"

"Honestly, I don't really know." She slips on a beige-colored shoe and adds, "I mean…my mother may be okay with it, but my father is an entirely different story. He's just temperamental, stubborn-headed, and annoyingly irrational sometimes. And since he's been trying out these new potions…*elixirs*, he's just worse than ever."

"How so?"

After she eases into the other shoe, she stands, and quietly replies, "It's all he thinks about, and I know he's only trying to find a way to protect us, but it's making him overly suspicious of *everyone*. He has all these locks and spellbound doors upstairs like he's afraid someone's going to run off with all the furniture or something. I don't know what it is, David, and it worries me."

I step closer to her and gently hold her face, so she'll look at me. "Hannah?"

"No, David. Don't try and tell me it's nothing because I know how bad things can get with my father. Uncle Elroy can tell you." She sucks in a shaky breath and adds, "My father and Elroy used to be very close a long time ago, but when Elroy met Savannah there was this absolute loathing, just a pure revulsion my father carried for her. One night, Uncle Elroy told my father they were leaving and wanted to start a new life somewhere else. My father did not give his gracious blessings, instead, an argument began between them. I wasn't there so I don't know what all was said, but they must've been going at it when the full moon set in. They changed and Savannah was caught in the fight. That next morning, my father stood over her dead body and told Elroy he got what he deserved for choosing the wrong blood."

My brain speeds through the images of Elijah and Elroy viciously battling it out, and then I lose my filter entirely and I blurt out, "Fuck! Your father killed Savannah?!"

"Yes, and he has no remorse for it whatsoever."

"Hannah, your father may not have been in control of himself. What he did was…" I have to refrain myself from saying every fucking foul word I can think of and go with, *"horrendous,* but I need you to listen to me, okay?"

She studies me briefly and finally mouths out, *"Okay."*

"The book Evan and I are looking for—"

She shoves my hands away. "Are you really going there now after what I just told you, David?"

I grip her shoulders and sternly say, "I am. This book opens up unknown portals allowing a demon to walk through. The one using this book can gain power by sacrificing others and collecting their blood. This demon's blood is like a drug. It can change you, making you addicted to it, so much so that you can't think of anything else. The more you drink— the more you will lose yourself. And yes, you can heal from wounds, you can move faster, you can become invisible to whomever you wish. This all may sound great, but you're also harming others in the process. And this is why Evan and I are searching high and low for this book."

"For you to use?" she demands.

I shake my head. "No. To destroy it."

"You think my father has it?"

"I know your father has it. Hannah, you said he's changed. If you want any good part of your father back, then we have to get it."

She jerks away like she's conflicted by my words and walks like she has the weight of the world bearing down on her. Every flower her hand skims by wilts, and the tone of the woods becomes gloomy and uninviting.

I offer my hand out to her, hoping to console her. "Hannah…"

"How are you so sure he has the book?"

I close my eyes and huff out, "Silas. He told me he brought the book to your father to—"

"To summon a demon?" she questions in a disbelieving tone.

"To have you. A way to seal the deal that you would belong to him."

She chokes out a halfhearted laugh. "I… I can't believe this. I don't want to believe this."

"I know," I reply dragging my eyes up to the treetops, guilt-ridden. I never wanted to be the one to tell her all this, but I had to.

"Do you know what this means?" she demands behind me.

I look over my shoulder and respond softly, "What?"

"I'll have to deceive my father, David. I'll have to come up with some kind of sneaky plan to search around. Do you know what he'd do to me if he figured out what I was up to?"

I shift to her and glide my thumbs along her chin trying to relieve the tension building inside her. She chews feverishly on her lower lip and I use the most comforting tone I have. "I'm not going to let anything happen to you. You want the same thing I do, protect the ones we love and that's exactly what we're going to do, okay?"

I feel the tension in her body unwind, her shoulders relax as she leans into me. "Before the next full moon, I may have a chance to find it."

––––––––––––––

As the weeks pass, Evan and I teach Hannah the sigils and what to look for that could be embedded in the demon's book. I can tell she's frightened, yet she's committed to saving her family. Each day she stops by after work and gives us an idea of how things are going on her end. Her father sticks to a rigid routine around the house, but the night before a full moon he leaves and goes out on the boat. And this will allow a moment of opportunity for her to search the upstairs. We're completely relying on Elijah's schedule. I know this makes Evan more uptight than usual but if anyone can break her father's spellbound doors and find the right keys to get in, it's Hannah. Tonight, Evan has the desk moved to the middle of the hotel room and the three of us gather around it like we're fixing to do a séance. The lights are dim and the T.V is off, and I lean back in my chair half expecting him to whip out tarot cards.

But instead, he eases against the desk and states in a humorless tone, "Hannah, if at any point you don't want to do this then David and I can rework the plan." He starts placing the maps he'd shown me before with the underground pathways. "We can take this section over here and it should lead us directly to the house…"

Hannah quickly examines the maps and says, "The passages are blocked, Evan. My father said they're too dangerous to have, and had them sealed off."

"Okay," Evan draws out with a heavy sigh.

"I can do this," Hannah boldly states glancing between me and Evan.

I slip my fingers through hers and reaffirm her words, "She can do this. You know better than us the layout of everything in the house. So, I have no doubt you'll find it." Hannah sends me a small smile and we stare at each other like Evan suddenly disappeared from the room. I closely watch as she looks over me, and I get the urge to lean over and kiss her tender lips.

But it vanishes away when I hear Evan grumble out, "You two wanna go get another room?" He moves from his chair and strides over toward the window. "I'm just giving you a hard time, David."

"Yeah, like you always do. It's part of your job description," I joke and cut a look his way.

I study the way his demeanor switches suddenly like he's bothered by something and then he asks, "Have you heard of anything else in the woods other than your kind, Hannah?"

"What do you mean?" she asks.

"I'm sure you know by now. David's probably told you. I've spent some time with Leah and the Nakoa family. One of her relatives mentioned a Goety to me. I had never heard the term before, and of course, I had to dig in deeper and find out what they were talking about. I finally convinced Leah to explain it to me. And let's just say, she wasn't very forthcoming. Apparently, she's very superstitious when it comes to speaking about it, but it's an evil spirit that's been seen throughout the town. Sometimes late at night, there's a sighting of a lost loved one roaming through the woods, and sometimes along the empty streets. Her friend Malcolm said he had actually experienced it himself when a cousin of his had recently died, and he saw her standing in his room. I'm not sure what this is or if it's just a figment of the imagination, but Leah's family definitely feels it's real." Evan turns and faces us and soberly asks, "Do you have any idea what this could be?"

Hannah nervously pushes a strand of hair behind her ear and replies, "*Ah….*" She lifts a shoulder lightly and adds, "I've heard the stories before, and I can obviously see why the Nakoa's would be unsettled by this. Who wouldn't be? The word is *wanaǵi* in their native tongue, but it basically means *ghost*." She changes her focus toward me, a remorseful look etches her expression. "To them, it's like an omen, but you have to understand there's a lot of idle talk around here mostly. None of it really reflects a favorable light on our family and I kinda feel like Grandmother Greta does… it's all the more reason for the Nakoa to hate us."

I stretch my arm across Hannah's chair. "Wolves, curses, witches, an evil spirit lurking around. *Yeah*, I can see that." I remark.

Evan strides back over, hands tucked inside his slacks as he calmly states, "We may not know the answers to everything, but I can assure you once we have the book, it'll be one less problem for all of us."

"As you can tell, Evan's not much of a multitasker. So, you can just imagine what his sex life is like," I quip.

Evan's glare darkens toward me. "This is the next topic you want to bring up, David? Really?"

Hannah practically leaps out of her chair, scoots it in, and states, "*Okay*. I really don't want to imagine anything regarding Evan or his personal life." She glances at Evan and sincerely adds in a lighter tone, "Sorry, Evan, if that sounded rude. It's nothing against you."

Evan turns off his scowling toward me and politely nods at Hannah. "No apology needed, Hannah. Besides, I think it's after David's bedtime." He takes his phone out and looks at it briefly. "Yup, it's seven-thirty. He gets really grumpy if he doesn't get enough sleep." His cocky smirk grows as he stares over to me.

"What? I don't go to bed at seven-thirty!" I snap.

The door to the hotel room opens and Evan and I glance back, Hannah's grabbing her things and sneaking out. "I think I'm going to let you two hash it out because I really have to get home now." Before she closes the door, I shift to her, sliding my hands along her neck and meet her awaiting lips. The kiss starts off slow, gentle— almost too gentle, and then the passion in us begins to ignite.

"Why?" Evan asserts shaking his head. "Why do I have to be a witness to this? The Gods are truly punishing me," he jokingly complains.

I take a second from her and remark back, "It's called love, Evan. You'll get there one day."

Chapter Twenty-One

Nothing changes for Hannah and me. Other than the fact that we're keeping our bond unknown. A subtle glance here or a faint touch there as she offers my coffee to me at the Witchery. I'm not sure how long we can keep this up because lifemates are usually inseparable, but under the circumstances, there's not much of a choice. The new moon will soon occur, and I can't shake the emotions I'm having. What if her father finds out about us, or her taking the book. What will he do? It's all just a stream of problems I try to solve in my head and none of it helps with the burning inferno inside me just waiting to unleash. Elements, they're a funny thing, they can be extremely useful, or if they're not handled right they can cause more harm than good.

I decide to take a ride out to the lake, maybe it will help clear my mind, but I find myself out in front of the Wolfenstein's house. There's not a soul in sight, just the towering trees bordering the gravel walkway. A tawny-colored squirrel scampers across the front porch as if he's warning the others of my presence. Hannah's father shouldn't be back for another hour, or so, and I still haven't picked up my jacket since the last time I was here. *Fuck it.* That's going to be my excuse. I turn my bike off and head toward the wooden screen door, but before I'm able to knock Catherine greets me. Her warm smile makes her look more motherly as she says, "David? You just missed dinner with the family." She wipes her hands off on her apron and welcomes me inside. "The girls didn't mention inviting anyone over."

"No. I was just dropping by to grab my jacket that I had left here," I say taking a step into the living room.

"Well, why don't you have a seat and I'll go round up some food for you. I'm sure you're hungry."

I raise a hand up and politely tell her I'm fine, "No need to go through any trouble, Catherine. I'm okay, really."

"You sure?" she asks walking toward the kitchen. The smell of peppermint and lavender flow through the air, and as I enter the area with her I note all the empty canning jars and jugs.

"I'm sure. I wanted to thank you again for dinner the other night, it was delicious," I reply picking up a jar. A huge, heavy pot sits on the stove, ribbons of hot steam drift out like serpents trying to escape the boiling water. "Are we canning something tonight?"

She lightly chuckles. "Oh, no. These are for Elijah. He's very, very nitpicky about his ritualistic tinctures. Everything has to be done in a particular way for all his tonics and remedies."

I place the jar back down. "I had no idea he practiced herbal medicine."

"Yes, he's always up to somethin'. Speaking of which, the girls are out on the dock," her voice wavers a bit as she quickly motions for me to follow her out to the back porch. "I'm sure they'll know where your jacket is. Oh, and David…I'm glad you enjoyed the dinner. You don't know how hard it is sometimes to cook a meal that will appeal to everyone."

"Well, thanks again," I cordially remark and journey toward the water. A cool breeze sweeps along the long wooden dock. A steady stream of clouds camouflage the evening sky, and I can see two figures sitting at the edge. Chloe and Jess look up as I approach.

"David, what are you doing here?" Chloe asks dipping her toes in the water.

Jess quickly unfastens her hair from a clip and lets the blonde waves flow down her back. "Did you miss us?" She bumps her arm against her sister and adds with a smirk, "He missed us, that's why he's out here, Chloe."

I shove my hands inside my pockets and reply, "I came by to grab my jacket actually." I motion toward the house. "Your mom said you two may know where it is."

Jess jumps to her feet, sauntering her way toward me. "You know, David…if you really," she states walking her fingers flirtatiously up my shirt, pausing her path as she continues with, "wanted to see us then all you had to do was—"

A splash of water hits Jess all along her backside, she spins around and yells at Chloe. "Hey!"

Chloe leans back wearing a satisfied grin. "I have your jacket, David."

Jess makes an attempt to fix her damp hair, and then as if a light flickered on inside her head she asks, "David, could you dry me off?" She bats her long lashes and makes a pleading expression pouting her lips, and sweetly begs, "Please?"

Another sudden splash of water hits Jess, and then Chloe waltzes toward us smiling like she just deviously outplayed her sister. "No. David doesn't have time for that, Jess. Didn't you hear? He needs his jacket, and I have it at my cabin. So…"

"So, Chloe you can just go get it for him," Jess promptly announces.

Chloe shoots an evil glare at Jess.

"Ladies, it's fine, really. I'll grab it on my way out," I state hoping to ease the tension between the two and walk out to the edge of the dock. I cast a glance over the placid dark lake and ask, "What are you two doing out here anyway? Water scrying tonight?"

Chloe dashes over and plops down first, and eagerly pats a board next to her. "Sit here with me, David."

Jess still carrying a scorned look toward her sister takes a seat on the other side of me. "Even if we did know how to scry in the waters our father wouldn't allow it," Jess explains somberly. I take a moment and look at her, she's leaned over, fingers gripping the edge of the old, weathered dock. The outline of her face shows affliction as she stares beyond the lake. "You know it's bad enough to know there's so much we can do with our magick, but what's worse is that we're cursed. And it doesn't matter what we do to try and change it— our family name will always be tainted with evil."

"Ahem…*Ah, Jess*? Let's lighten the mood a bit, okay?" Chloe urges and bumps her shoulder against me.

"So, David, I really like your shirt it brings out the green in your eyes. Makes you look dreamier."

Jess snorts. "Dreamier? Really, Chloe?" She brushes her hand along my jeans. "I would say he looks more tempting."

"Dreamier, tempting the same thing," Chloe asserts as she glides her hand down my other leg.

I quickly grab both wandering hands and place them back on their laps. "All right, all right…you two are awfully handsy tonight. Besides where's Elijah or Hannah?"

Jess drums her fingers along the rugged boards and nods out toward the lake. "Out there."

I narrow my gaze and ask, "They're in the water?"

"No, they're on the boat," Jess says in a hushed tone.

Chloe dips her feet in the liquid darkness beneath the dock, and as she splashes the water over her toes, she explains, "It's one of those talks father gives if he feels like we're straying from the path."

"Who's straying from the path?" I ask.

Jess rolls her eyes. "Who do you think?"

Silence lingers around us for a beat and then Jess bends forward, meeting her sister's eyes. "He doesn't see it," she whispers.

Chloe faces me with a serious look. "Don't you think Hannah's a little strange? I mean besides the fact she's always nose deep in a book and—"

"No. Why would I think she's strange?" I interrupt.

"Creepy is more like it. Right, David?" Jess goads with a simple nod.

Chloe snaps her fingers. "Yes, but ghastly sounds more fitting."

"Dreadful," Jess chimes in arching a brow.

"*And gross*," both utter at the same time.

I scan Chloe's face first and then slowly scan Jess' face. My expression must say it all, because I'm confused and kinda taken back by the way they're acting. Jess scoots closer and gently pats my leg likes she's trying to console me. "I know, David, it has to be hard to see past our beauty…no wait gorgeousness. That's what you called me when we first met, remember? anyway—"

"No, he was implying that to both of us, Jess. Not just *you*," Chloe intrudes.

"Whatever," Jess brushes her off as if her words mean nothing to her and continues, "Hannah…is kinda like the runt of our small little litter here even though she's the oldest. She was born with this trait, now mind you, our mother tried to say it was a gift. *Pfft*."

"It's gross and—" Chloe mouths out but Jess quickly cuts her off.

"*Hush*, Chloe. I'm trying to get to that! Anyway, when she was like eight or nine things got creepier. People around the town kept saying they saw someone that had passed away. Their aunt, uncle, brother, friend, neighbor, whoever would just show up in their house or walking along a wooded path. Chloe and I thought it all was just gibberish until we saw it happen here. A friend's mother had died, we remembered her only because she would walk him to school each day. I'm not sure why she died really, but after the funeral the next night we saw her again. Alive. She just strolled right up to our house, up the staircase, and crawled right into Hannah's bed. Of course, Chloe screamed her head off."

"So did you!" Chloe sasses back.

Jess presses a finger against her lips and scowls. "*Shh*, do you mind? I'm telling a story. We ran and told our parents, but it was Grandmother Greta that knew what was wrong before anyone else did. She had said Hannah was a walker, a spirit walker. You know…like a sleep walker but instead, Hannah walks in her sleep impersonating the dead."

"Creepy," Chloe voices softly.

"Gross, right, David?" Jess questions eyeing me. "Come on, you have to admit beauty can only go so far. And there's a line drawn when you're sleeping next to someone, and the next thing you know you could be staring at someone from an obituary you just read about that day. Believe me, David, it is not romantic or comforting in any way."

Chloe adds pointing toward the lake, "That's why Hannah and our father are out on the boat tonight. She hasn't had any episodes in a while until recently. A few nights ago someone told our father what she saw, and he knew immediately it was Hannah."

"Our dead girl straying from the path," Jess mumbles softly.

"Stop it, Jess. What if mother heard you say that? Besides it's—"

"Gross," Jess adds to Chloe's words.

Both girls laugh and smile like little deviants and I'm starting to wonder if what they're telling me is true. "*Wait*...how do I know you're not just telling me this to make me not like Hannah?"

"Oh! See, Jess I told you I thought he liked her," Chloe exclaims.

"Well, I'm afraid to say, David, these girls know exactly what they're talkin' about," a gruff voice announces from behind us. I turn around and find Elroy standing a few feet away. Chloe and Jess hop up, their bare feet glisten with water.

"Uncle Elroy. We were just telling David about Hannah's gift," Chloe states in a chaste like tone.

"Uh huh, sure you were," he retorts and spits crudely out toward the lake. "I'd better not hear you call your sister that again, ya hear?"

He takes a step closer and Jess bends down a bit trying to wring out the water from her dress. "We didn't mean anything by it, Uncle Elroy," Jess explains as she hesitates with a phony smile.

He spits again before he says roughly, "Why don't you two head on back to your cabins now. You don't want your daddy to know you were out here this late, do ya?"

"No," both girls reply in unison.

As Chloe leads a path down the rickety dock, she stops and turns. "Oh. Ah, David…do you want your jacket?"

I'm up on my feet, standing just to the side of Elroy and before I have the chance to reply he says, "I'll get it for him on his way out, Chloe. No need to worry that pretty little head of yours. Go on now."

She slowly turns back around but I can tell she wants to say something else but decides against it. I watch as her and Jess trail off to their cabins, each treading with heavyhearted steps like they were scolded and confined to their rooms. I've always felt the sisters had a good-humored nature about them, maybe a bit much on the flirty side, but tonight, something troubled Jess. I rehash what Jess had said about Hannah being a *spirit walker*. It's not uncommon for witches to have different abilities. Some may not even know what their innate powers are until they're much older. But Hannah was already using this ability since she was a child from what Chloe and Jess had said.

"I imagine you have some questions about Hannah now," Elroy interrupts my thoughts as he strides closer. We're face to face, he's so close I can smell the scent of cigarettes reeking from him. "I'll have you know. Jess and Chloe are good girls they just yap too damn much. Hannah though…" he laughs and walks to the edge of the pier. "She is an unusual sort but I'm not out here to sway you, David. Being bound to someone doesn't put a stop on those deeply-rooted feelings or perhaps those second thoughts you might be havin'. Now does it?"

"Second thoughts? What are you talking about, Elroy? And how do you know we're bound?" I ask.

He looks off in the distance, staring at the darkness that seems to stretch out forever, and idly replies, "I know plenty, boy. I also know when to keep my mouth shut. C'mon, let's head on up before Elijah and Hannah get back."

He slips out a pack of smokes from the pocket of his red flannel shirt and gestures a nod for me to follow. A cig hangs between his lips as he taps the end and lights it. One touch is all it takes for him to conjure his own fire. Making it look like it's mere child's play. We walk to Chloe's cabin and I wait by the gravel path while he retrieves my jacket. As soon as we turn to leave Chloe's cabin lights flicker off one by one until it's completely dark inside. Elroy hands the jacket to me with a crooked smile. "These girls, they're somethin' else I tell ya." He steals a drag and eases a hand in his pocket and starts walking. "I don't want you to get the wrong notion about Hannah, David. It's not at all like how the girls tell it— like it's a dead, rotten corpse traipsing around scarin' folks."

"Okay…" I remark waiting for him to clarify more.

He inhales deeply and cuts a side glance toward me. "Hannah has a good heart, a good soul. She's not out to get anybody, but the thing is… it's unsettling for folks to lose someone and then hours or days later see them reappear. She can take on their mortal form in every way and she's aware she's doing it. Here's the deal, David. She thinks she's givin' them peace of mind so to speak. A ghostly figure reachin' for ya trying to sputter out everything's goin' to be fine, but I can't fathom one person that would sit around long enough to hear those consoling words. I mean, would you?"

"I… I don't know," I mumble.

"Well, it's not an easy thing to handle that's for sure," he says veering off the path. He waves the cigarette back and forth. "When my lifemate passed on I'd never thought I'd see her again, but about three nights after I heard the damn floorboards creak and groan just as I was about to fall asleep. I rolled over to my side, and there standin' just a foot away from the bed was my Savannah. For a split second, I thought I was dreamin'. So, I sat up in bed and wondered if I had gone mad or somethin' but then she spoke and every cotton-picking hair on my body stood straight up." He halts his steps and looks in my direction. His narrow eyes widen, his lips twitch and I can tell the moment still catches him off-kilter.

The rough gravel beneath my boots crunch as I turn to face him and ask, "What did she say to you?"

He blinks and quietly says, "She said…that she will always love me and that she'd protect me." He tosses his cig down and quickly runs a hand over his eyes and starts walking again. "I jumped out of my bed and followed her all the way to Hannah's cabin. I watched her crawl in bed, and then her form reshaped itself. The next thing know, I was lookin' at Hannah." We make our way along the thin trail to his front porch. He slouches down on the upper step and says in an indifferent tone, "You know the first thing Hannah said to me when I woke her up?"

"What's that?"

"She was sorry." He takes another smoke out, taps the end of the rolled-up tobacco, and adds, "It was like magick at its finest, flawless, natural, just as easy as puttin' on your best bib and tucker. And Hannah knew what she was doin' the whole time. Now was it gut-wrenching? I won't lie to ya, yeah it was, but creepy, naw. Maybe it's because I understood why she was doin' it, David."

"So you don't believe she was doing it to scare you?"

His dark brows furrow in frustration as he replies, "No. She was only tryin' to give me some sort of peace. You have no idea what it's like to lose a lifemate, do you?" He props a scraggly hand on one knee and purses his lips. "Why, boy, do I get the feelin' you have no formulation of what I'm talkin' bout?"

I rest a boot on a warped, creaky step and say, "All right then, enlighten me."

His whole body moves as he chuckles to himself and droops his head down. "She sees the dead for what they are, their past, how they died, who they loved, and most importantly she can mirror whatever she sees fit. Now with her being blood bound her powers could possibly intensify if you get my drift?"

"I think I get it, but why is she out with Elijah tonight?"

He flicks an ash to the side and retorts coldly, "Why? I'll tell ya why… cus if it raises attention to us then you better bet your ass he's gonna take care of it." He leans back and huffs out a billow of smoke. "It's all about my brother. It always has been. The all-knowin' Elijah, the proud, the swelled-head, patronizing bastard, and if it doesn't deliver him the powers from the gods or, whatever, then it *will be* swept under a rug. Take it from me, son. I should know."

"Who else knows about me and Hannah?" I ask.

He coughs harshly into his hand and then sucks in another slow drag. "Other than me? No one. There's been too much fuss goin' on with the Nakoa and their damn shit to even worry about anything else." A shroud of smoke whispers from his mouth as an image materializes. A lone faded wolf races through the veil of lingering fumes. He sits still for a moment with his eyes closed, and eventually spouts, "I think it's best you better head on back now before they get home."

"Yeah, you're probably right," I agree and start to move away.

I hear him call out to me, "David… Hannah's the one that's goin' to need the protectin' ya hear?" He points up toward the cloudy sky, hints of the partial moon come into view, but just as quickly, it's hidden from my sight. I get what he means and give him a subtle nod.

178

Chapter Twenty-Two

I meet Evan at a place known as Grotto's Bar and Grill downtown. It's tightly wedged in between two other buildings but doesn't seem to deter anyone. It's small, cramped, and exclusive. As I enter I notice there's barely enough room to slip through each table. Evan waves me over as he sits at the bar. A huge, wood-fired grill is stationed on the far side and an entire wine rack on the other filled with different tinted bottles. Considering how small the place is it's not lacking patrons tonight. The room flits with laughter, while voices carry over each other and there's no telling what's in the drinks. Shot glasses to martini glasses line a natural stone bar. A full-bosomed, redheaded woman waits on a couple seated next to us. Before she ventures off, she asks, "Hiya, sweets. What can I get ya?"

I glance over to Evan's drink and reply, "A shot of whatever he's having."

"You sure?" she questions holding two empty wine glasses.

I raise a curious brow. "Yeah?"

She edges closer to us and in a slight whisper says, "It's the stout stuff here. None of that watered-down beer and wine. More of a true witch's drink." She smiles and slips back. "So, two witch's brews comin' up then?"

Evan taps the bar and replies, "Yes, Gemma. I think you have it."

I swivel around in my chair and eye Evan. "Wait a minute. You know Gemma?"

"Yeah? Why?"

"Doesn't she own a library here?" I ask.

"Why would she own a library?"

I prop my elbows on the bar and lower my voice. "The girls had mentioned they had an Aunt Gemma, while Hannah was watching the library one day while she was out."

"Well, you might get your answer because look who just walked in," Evan states, and in a breath everything in me changes. My pulse quickens to a soft, steady hum, and courses through my blood-hot veins. I turn and catch Hannah hedging along the stone sculpted walls. She steers clear of the customers and vanishes through an indirect access. A door carved and obscured from most, but it's used for the employees to enter and go through. Just to the side is an actual grotto with a spring running through it. A blue light hangs above, making the scene an unworldly, cavern-like setting.

"Two brews for my fellow comrades," Gemma blurts placing our drinks down.

Evan grins and tips his glass toward Gemma. "Thanks."

I ease over and take mine and ask, "I didn't know Hannah worked here."

Gemma flicks her long, crimson hair back and braces her hands against the bar. "She doesn't. We're short-handed tonight. How do you know her?"

"The library," I remark taking a drink.

"Oh, well then she's your girl when it comes to literature." Gemma curves her slender body downward like she's grabbing something beneath the bar and slaps a bundle of books in front of us. "She's constantly hounding me for stuff like this." She offers me a cheerful smile and juts her shapely chin out. "Whatever helps when you have enemies barking at your door, I'd say."

Evan and I both swing our gaze in the opposite direction and three tables over are Malcolm, Greg, Leah, and a host of others. Leah's dark hair is pulled back in a high ponytail. Her black shirt and leather pants make her look more uptight and rebellious. As they talk, Hannah strides up. Her vanilla perfume hits me before I lock eyes with her. "David? Wh-what are you doing here?"

"He's just havin' a drink, Hannah. You know how boys are. Oh, and by the way, here's those books you were looking for," Gemma placidly states.

Hannah eagerly grips the books, but before she moves away I reach out and touch her fingers. It's not noticeable to some, but the fire between us blazes inside. Our eyes stay locked to each other and I can feel her breathing shiver like she's on the verge of losing it.

"Evan, you didn't tell me your traveling buddy was into blondes." Gemma teases and hands Hannah a rag. "Before you forget we have more than one customer here. May I suggest you start wiping down the bar, Hannah?"

Hannah blushes and turns away. "Yeah, that might be a good idea, Gemma." She drags her fingers through her hair and wanders slowly to the other side stacking the books in a safe place.

"Well…well, look what we have here…" Leah voices loudly. She presses herself in between me and Evan and smiles from ear to ear. "Two from the Wolfenstein family and it's barely even a full moon yet, Greg. How fucking lucky are we?" she questions dramatically slapping the bar with her hand.

Greg and Malcolm stand quietly behind us. Gemma smirks and rests a hand on her hip. "What can I help you with, Leah?"

"I want that blondie over there to bring us another round," Leah remarks. Hannah cuts a look over her shoulder.

"She's busy. Let me bring over whatever you need," Gemma generously offers but Hannah's already carrying a pitcher of beer.

She marches by Gemma and nonchalantly says, "I got it, Gemma."

Leah grips our arms and holds us close together. "See, that's what I'm talkin' about. You gotta show them who's the chief around here, boys."

Hannah begins pouring their drinks as each takes a seat. The conversation fades around the table. A beefed-up guy with arms bigger than my thighs pipes up, "What's she doing here?"

Leah stabs at a piece of food on her plate. "I asked for her to come serve our drinks to us. You have a problem with that Jansen?"

He grabs his drink, peers inside it briefly and replies, "Nope. I don't have a problem checking her out while she serves me tonight." He swallows down his beer and motions for Hannah to come closer. "I'll have another… *please*," he taunts showcasing a cocky grin. Hannah quietly pours another as everyone at the table watches with growing interest.

His eyes start to scan over her body, but Leah intervenes sharply with, "Careful, Jansen. You know what they say about the Wolfenstein girls."

Hannah penetrates a look toward Leah. Suddenly the entire room feels smaller, voices that belted out before seemingly die away and the air is thick with hostility. "What's the word about the Wolfenstein girls now, Leah?" Hannah questions striding around the table.

Leah leans back and dangles her arm over the chair. A slow, greedy smirk curves at her lips. "Oh, you know. The usual. I personally don't think any of that will change because we all know what little cock-teasers your sisters are."

"Oh, Leah," Hannah scoffs, unfazed by Leah's comment, and stands by her chair. "There is one thing I would like to know?"

Leah peers up, her overbold smile spreads as she remarks, "Oh, yeah? What's that?"

"Are you finished with your plate?"

A confused look riddles over Leah's face but then she quickly gathers herself and sasses, "Yeah, and on your way back tell Evan and his brother to come join us."

"Sure thing," Hannah politely remarks removing the plate. She takes her time walking toward the bar. There's no trace she's bothered by Leah and her harassing words. Matter-of-fact, my own body feels oddly comfortable and tranquilized.

Gemma wipes a pilsner glass out and whispers over to Hannah, "Don't let them get to you, hon. You know they're always just mouthing."

"I'm not," she whispers back and looks over to me. "I think you have an invite at a table over there."

Gemma quietly chuckles. "The Nakoa are constantly making trouble in some way or another like they have nothing else better to do." She angles her body with her back facing Leah and her rowdy group and winks over to Evan. "Don't look so antsy. They won't bite."

Evan glares toward me. "Think you can keep your fire from burning anything down, David?"

"Hey, if anything goes wrong, I've got a nifty fire extinguisher that I nicknamed The Quencher, and for added reassurance, we just installed a new sprinkler system," Gemma reveals sarcastically.

"Are you saying I can't keep my—"

"Your shit together? Yes, that's what I'm implying, David," Evan states as he eases away from the barstool. As we reach Leah's table they move chairs around so we can sit, Greg and Malcolm both greet us with a short nod. Everyone, including Leah, wears a silver ring much like the one Evan had bought from her family shop. I study the Jansen guy closely. Every nerve and muscle in me twitches with adrenaline. I saw the way he was looking over Hannah and the way he was speaking to her. He might even think he was putting on a damn good show, bullshitting everyone else, but deep down he wants her.

"I'm guessing you two had a relapse?" Leah inquires.

Evan swirls the bright green liquor around in his mug and offers a lopsided frown. "I just can't seem to keep David on track. It is tough I have to say…" Evan flashes a cunning look toward me. "But I think there's still hope."

I grunt and play along. "Well… if there were other things to do here I wouldn't have a problem."

Malcolm pushes his plate to one side and suggests, "There's a place I know of just east of town, bet that would keep your mind from wanting a drink."

"Really?" I ask. "What's so special about this place?"

"Malcolm…what are you doing?" Leah roughly whispers. "You don't wanna know, David. Besides haven't you heard the news about the couple that went missing?"

Evan's interest is piqued as he sits forward more and asks, "What couple?"

Leah tightens her ponytail and discreetly scans the room. "It was tourists, you know how we get flooded with them during the festivals. It's sad to say, but sometimes it happens. They get lost in the woods or whatever, but usually family and friends start getting worried, and of course, they call the local police to have it checked out."

"Was this recently?" Evan asks.

She scrunches her face and peeks over to Malcolm. "It's been a few weeks ago, right?"

"Yeah, I think so," he quickly retorts back.

Leah suddenly grips Evan's hand and gives him the strangest expression. Her dark, round eyes stare into his and I can't help wondering why she's laying it on a little thick.

"Evan, maybe it's not a good idea to check this place out. Okay?"

I almost bust out laughing when Evan returns with, "*Okay...*"

Her face glazes over with resentment. It's apparent it's not the response she was hoping for. "Why don't I get you another one of those drinks you're having?" she asks leisurely rubbing her hand along his arm and up to his shoulder. "You're kinda tense tonight."

Gemma saunters by, drops another mug down and smiles. "Got ya covered, Evan." Her silk-like tone holds no competitive edge, but even if it did, there wouldn't be a need. Gemma's red hair hangs in curls just above her cleavage. She carries herself in an entirely different light compared to Leah. Charming, high-toned, and clever. When I look at Leah all I see is a tomboyish girl, toting around a bag full of arrows, *but then again*, maybe I'm just biased.

"Gemma…*Gemma*, my girl. What have you been up to?" Jansen says.

"What? You have to be kidding me, Jansen. You honestly believe I have time to do anything else outside this place?" Gemma jokingly replies and grabs Evan's empty mug.

Jansen places his elbows on the table and steeples his fingers together like he's taking her all in. "Why don't you come out with us tonight, after you close the place up and bring that niece of yours too if you want?"

I lean my own elbow on the table and rub the light stubble along my face. "I think her niece has plans, sorry buddy," I coldly remark.

Evan inhales deeply and gulps down the rest of his drink. Leah stops her flirting with Evan and bounces a curious look from Jansen to me.

"How would you know, David, that her niece has plans later?" Leah asks stretching her arm over the back of Evan's chair. She reminds me of a spiteful mistress of corruption with the way she scowls over to me. The side of her full lower lip slants a bit like she's trying to read my mind. I'm betting she wishes she could right about now, but I answer before she has a chance to mouth off something else.

"Last time I checked it's not a crime to ask someone out."

Evan clears his throat and quickly adds, "I think Hannah and David were talking at the bar earlier and—"

"He asked her out, yeah, *yeah* I got it, but she's not the type of girl I pictured David with. *C'mon*, she's a Wolfenstein. There is a reason why nobody asks them out." Her forehead scrunches upward as her brows lift. It makes her look much older than she is and there's only two words I can use to describe her look, utterly appalled.

"You know she has a crazy-ass father?" Leah goads, it sounds like a question but it's a stab at the family, nonetheless.

"Enough, Leah," Gemma snaps. "I don't think you have any room to talk."

"Oh, forgive me, am I stepping on your family's toes?" Leah mocks and smirks at Malcolm.

Greg crosses his arms over his chest and calmly says, "See why we come here? There's always action and conflict." He rolls his eyes toward Leah. "C'mon, Leah. Let's just drop it and go."

Malcolm and Greg both stand and leave. My impression of them alters a smidge only because they know when to throw in the towel. But Jansen, he's still sitting contently watching us go back and forth. I catch him out of the corner of my eye easing back every so often looking for Hannah. Gemma grips ahold of my shoulder and softly says, "If you need anything else, you'll know where I am." She completely avoids Leah keeping her sight forward and walks to another table.

"Hey… *hey*…I wasn't finished talking to you!" Leah shouts as Gemma goes on attending to the other customers. There's only a handful left. Most seem to have disappeared once Leah started her ranting. She cranes her head toward Evan. "I swear the service here sucks! C'mon Evan, let's get out of here. You could use a little midnight stroll. What do you say?"

"What about the tourists? Doesn't that put a damper on things?" Evan asks.

"Look they just got lost, that's all. If you haven't lived here all your life then, yeah, the woods can be hard to figure out," Leah states in a carefree tone. "Who knows, maybe we'll find them, and we'll be heroes," she laughs and rises from her chair. "I'll be outside if you change your mind."

While Evan guzzles down the last of his drink, I mosey on over to the bar and send a quick text message. Evan peers at me stumped as he walks over and asks, "What's this?"

"Alcoholic anonymous hotline, they're available twenty-four-hours," I remark.

"Three drinks and now I'm hammered?" I shrug as Evan pats my back and says, "Nice to know you care, David."

"Well, I can't have you stumbling out of here. Leah might take advantage of you, Ev."

Evan scoffs. "We can't have none of that now, can we?"

Gemma threads her hands together and leans over the bar. "You two aren't really brothers are you?"

I grin at Evan. "What do you mean? We're like peas in a pod, aren't we, Evan?"

"More like night and day."

"Oh, yeah. I'm the dark, mysterious, don't forget *handsome* brother. And you're…" I tilt my head sideways and eye him before I go on, "the mind-numbing, drunk."

He holds up his fingers and retorts, "Three drinks, David. Just three."

Gemma smiles. "Okay… I think I get it." She points between us and says, "You're coven brothers." Evan quietly nods.

A chair screeches back and Jansen wanders our way. He steers himself to the barstool next to me and asks, "You guys gonna head out to that place later?"

"I don't know, why?" I reply.

He waits a beat, scratches the side of his face, and says, "Somethin' to do. I think Gemma's gonna close up soon and maybe she'll tag along if you guys come."

Gemma moves away, her smile lessens. "The only place I'm going to after work is home. Sorry."

Jansen snags a napkin and asks, "Got a pen?"

Gemma huffs out a loud sigh and slips out a pen form the pocket of her blouse and tosses it on the bar. "Look, if you're planning on giving me your number, then don't bother because I'm kinda seeing someone." She takes Evan's hand and sweetly offers, "Let me show you the rest of the place before we close."

Evan doesn't look as shocked as I thought he would, sneaky bastard. He's had his eye on her apparently for a while now. I watch amused as she leads him to the back and I yell out, "Don't worry about the rest of the customers, Gemma. I'll take care of it!" When I check around me though, every table is empty, leaving me and Jansen the only two left. Jansen scribbles something down on the napkin and folds it up.

I aim my thumb toward it and ask, "What's that?"

"I wasn't going to leave my number for Gemma," Jansen remarks.

"Who's it for?"

He combs his fingers through his slicked-back hair like he's fixing himself up for someone. Bobbing his head side to side staring at the mirror behind the bar. "It's for the blonde."

"You mean, Hannah?" I ask.

"Yeah, listen…I don't know what you think you *might* have with her, but you're just a drifter. And if you had a one-night stand then I understand, but it's nothing more than just that."

"Oh, yeah?"

He chuckles and I chuckle right along with him. He reaches for a glass that's half-full and I mentally move it. It's just enough so he'll have to stretch out to get it. Jansen glances at me with an impassive look and tries again. The glass slides away like it's being tugged by an invisible string. Persistently, he makes another attempt and this time I let it fly across the bar. It lands on the floor and shatters apart.

"What the fuck?" Jansen stammers out. "Did you see that?"

"See what?"

"The glass…it…"

"Sounds like you've had one too many, Jansen. I think it's time for you to go home," I state stiffly.

"But…" he mumbles easing carefully off his barstool.

As he bends down to inspect the broken pieces I use my ability with a little more force and swing the main door open. Jansen jumps and spins around. His face turns as white as a ghost. He stands gripping the bar and sputters, "What's going on?"

I hop off the barstool and calmly reply, "Like I said, Jansen. It's probably best for you to head on home."

He does a doubletake of the glass and the door and then creeps over to a table. "*Yeah…maybe I should…*" he takes another timid step and then another slinking closer to the entrance. He practically tiptoes around the last table and then runs out. As soon as he disappears I slam the door closed and take a seat. I drag over his napkin and crumble it in my hand and set it on fire.

"What's that smell?" Hannah questions as she approaches the bar.

"What smell?" I answer hoping she'll believe me.

"It smells like something burning…" She drops her gaze to my hand, tendrils of smoke seep through my fingertips. "David?"

"Oh, you mean this?" I let the ashes fall from my grasp and smile. "I was just taking care of something."

"Uh huh," she playfully mocks and caresses her hand over mine. Stray blonde ringlets curve around her heart-shaped face. The rest fall as she unpins her hair from the tan bandana. "Sorry, I probably look like a mess. I was helping Aunt Gemma with the dishes back there."

I lick my lips and reply, "You know…I could—"

"Help with the dishes? *That's right* you know your way around a kitchen," she chuckles.

"No, what I was going to say is I could take you right here."

Her cheeks redden and before she glances away I shift around the bar in a blink. She lets out a surprised breath and whispers, "David…I'm a mess."

"I don't care. I wouldn't care if you're lathered up in soap or drenched in mud I would still want you because you know why? You're mine."

"Are you trying to sweet talk me, so I won't drag you back there and make you do the dishes?" she asks running her fingertips over my lips.

I gently kiss her fingers and reply, "I might."

My hands travel down to her hips and I lift her up to the bar. She leans in and presses her mouth to mine. I could stay like this with her forever, feeling how tender and intimate she touches me. Every simple kiss commands more until I have my hands tangled in her hair. I break free and trail my lips along her neck.

Tasting her soft skin, smelling her sweet scented perfume and it drives me crazy.

"Hey, guys…*ah*…" Gemma's voice suddenly calls out. "Oh, gosh. I'm so sorry."

I stay nuzzled up to Hannah and grumble, "It's okay." I slowly pull back and spot Gemma by the end of the bar. She covers her face like she's uncomfortable.

"Is it okay to look," Gemma asks.

Hannah laughs. "You act like we were naked. Yes, you can uncover your eyes now."

Gemma waltzes over and grins like she just caught two teenagers getting it on. "Sorry, I've just never seen you smooching and nuzzling up with someone like that." She flicks the backlights out as Evan shifts in.

He steals a moment, glances around, and asks, "David, where's Jansen?"

"Oh…" I clear my throat. "He had to go home."

"Really? That's too bad," Evan replies nonchalantly.

"Speaking of home, Hannah, I better drop you off before you turn into a pumpkin…*no* wait, a wolf," Gemma grins wiping the bar off.

"Gemma!" Hannah scolds and hops down.

"What? You think these guys don't have a clue who or what we are by now?" Gemma questions and tosses the rag in a bin. "We're the talk of the town and they use that to make profit off of us. All the phony witch stuff they hang in their display windows and trinket shops."

"I take it since you showed Evan around he knows why you set this place up?" Hannah asks.

"She has a healing spring here," Evan states and aims toward the indoor grotto.

"Wait, a healing spring and you serve booze?" I ask puzzled.

"Yeah, why not?" Gemma retorts like it's no big thing. "Next time you come to town I'll throw us a little private dinner party, okay?" I look over to Evan and I can already tell he has the hots for her.

"Sounds good," Evan says.

"All right guys, I need to get this girl home," Gemma announces and starts turning the rest of the lights off.

Hannah pulls on my shirt and lightly kisses me. "I'll see you tomorrow."

Chapter Twenty-Three

I'm standing with Evan on the corner of the street. A metal lantern hangs from the bar's entrance. The glass is so old it's stained yellow making everything look gloomy and lifeless. "Tell me again why you didn't want to take Gemma back to her place?"

"Did you not hear her say, she had to take Hannah home?" Evan questions in a disgruntled voice.

"I could have taken her home," I state.

"What, two hours later?"

"I could have taken her back to our room. It's not like she's under lock and key."

"Okay, let's say you did take Hannah home, and when you rode up on your bike with her father sitting on the front porch, *what then*?" Evan challenges wearing a know-it-all smirk.

I shut my mouth because he has a point. An uneasy stillness meanders along the barren roads. All the stores are bunkered down for the night, and I notice it's not quite a full moon. The grim clouds still embrace the sky like it's withholding information.

"Should I give you a little more time to work out the constellations, or are you coming?" Evan elbows me.

"Oh, yeah. I was just wondering if it's going to rain," I finally answer and step off the curb.

"Looks like it might, so we better hurry." He jogs across the street and waits for me to catch up.

"Where are we going, Ev?"

"To that place, Leah was talking about."

———————

We hike through the woods for a good thirty minutes. If we knew the place better we'd shift to the area. That's the only bad thing about shifting unless you're a first-timer. I remember Marc learning how to do it. Dawson explaining, shifting is natural for us, this is the way motion is created in our world. You're shifting from one parallel reality to another parallel reality, eventually, you're doing this by your own second nature. So, the question isn't can you shift, it's where will you shift to? Evan's voice cuts in my reminiscing from back in the day.

"You're awfully quiet back there, you okay?"

"Yeah, just wondering why you didn't take the chance to get laid tonight," I mouth climbing up a steep ridge.

"And this concerns you in what way?"

"I'm not concerned," I dryly reply meeting him beside a tree, gripping it I scan around.

He laughs. "Could have fooled me, besides, Gemma and Hannah had other things to do. Just like we have other things to do."

"Like we had to scout out this woodsy place in the middle of the night to get our nocturnal exercise?"

"Something like that, come on. We're almost there." Evan urges with a quick nod.

"If Gemma's their aunt that would make her Elijah's sister, right?" I ask.

Evan dodges a low hanging limb. "No. She's Catherine's sister. Interesting that you brought up Elijah though. Gemma mentioned she had begged Catherine not to marry him."

"So they're not lifemates?"

"No, and from what I understand he doesn't believe in that. She said that he started off in water scrying, candle magick to even using snakes in some kind of witch sermon before the full moon. None of it sated him and he went on to performing black magick, and now we know he's taken it a step further and possesses a demon book."

"Wow. He soared through the basics and jumped headfirst into the dark arts. Pretty ballsy."

The woods thicken and the overshadow from the clouds makes our vision limited. "David…can you give us some light?"

I call on my element and form an orb of fire in my palm. "Better?"

"Yes, at least we can see where we're going," Evan affirms weaving through the trees.

"Want me to hold your hand?"

"What? No," he remarks sharply.

My shirt snags on a branch and as I yank it free with my other hand I catch something marked inside the tree. "Evan?"

"Yeah?"

"Come take a look at this." I rub my fingers over the markings. A cut that's so deep the tree still oozes sap down the edges of its bark.

"It's a sigil," Evan states and grabs my arm. "Back up." He pivots around carefully observing the space we're in. "Did you see any more like this on our way up here?"

"No."

Evan launches into his GI Joe mode and starts canvassing every tree. A twig snaps under my boot and the next thing I see is a hand. Evan's wordless command to stay still. He walks to another tree about five feet away and then waves me over. I feel like we're in enemy territory waiting to be ambushed. If the wind blows suddenly we both look in that immediate direction. I roam quietly behind Evan until he halts beside a large oak. "Shine some light here," he says in a low voice. I raise my hand up and make out another sigil. It's cut the same, but the design is different. We move on with stealth and vigilance making sure we don't draw attention to ourselves.

Nearly ten paces out I walk right into a spider's web. I shake off the sticky net and gently maneuver around the arachnid. My fiery orb illuminates a third sigil deeply carved into a tree, each one so far is distinct and prominent. "Evan,…found another one." I trace the mark and feel an odd, burning sensation swarm inside my bones.

Evan sneaks up beside me. "We could be standing inside a circle. You know that, right?"

"Or we could be standing on the outskirts of it," I reply.

"There's only one way to tell. Shine over there," Evan instructs keeping his voice faint. I carry my fire farther out and expand the flames across our path. The circumference of the three sigils show a silhouette of a witch's circle. It's arched away from us and I tentatively turn toward Evan and say, "We're not inside it."

Evan agrees with a brisk nod and we begin patrolling the rest of the area. Our footsteps become muffled with the help from the bed of pine needles blanketing the ground. It's so eerily quiet the only sound I can hear is a high-pitched ringing in my ears. The deeper we tread the darker it gets, and the bizarre sensation I had fizzles out. I let my shoulders relax and suck in a steady breath. I'm so keyed-up I could roast anything that walked in front of me. Evan abruptly seizes my upper arm and says, "Stop. There's something on the ground…"

I stare into the dark and shrouded woods and see a body lying flat. Long scarlet hair flutters listlessly across a pale face. Her maimed arms are stretched outward and there's not a twitch or even a flinch as

Evan moves closer. I ease in and realize there's blood soaked along her torn jeans and shoes.

"It's Devon," Evan says crouching down.

I hover my fire around us making sure we're alone. "What happened to her?"

Evan brushes the knotted strands of hair from her face. Her tear-filled eyes widen and her lips tremble with fear. "*I...I c-can't* move," she stammers.

"What happened, Devon?" Evan asks.

"I was… bitten …" she mouths wearily.

"By what? What bit you, Devon?" Evan keeps the timber of his voice calm and even.

"A snake…" She looks up to me and pleads, "*David*...help me, please. *I... I* can't move my body."

"Okay, we're going to try and help you." Evan stands and says over his shoulder, "We need to get her out of here. I'm not sure—"

As the words suddenly falter from his mouth I know we're no longer alone. Off in the distance, there's a woman in white, standing perfectly still as if she were nailed to the ground. Blonde curls whisk over her shoulders as the wind picks up, and the soil beneath our feet violently shakes. Dirt, rocks, and roots thrust out of the earth, and then a gaping hole forms. Devon's paralyzed body falls in. She screams and Evan drops to his knees and reaches for her, but it's too late, she's gone. The earth seals itself back up and her body is dragged underground as the surface rolls like massive waves. Roots crack and the stones below grind. Evan and I watch in shock as the woman in white slowly turns away. Her flowing dress blends in with the darkness and her figure vanishes.

Evan cranes his head toward me. "You sure Hannah went home?"

"Ah…yeah" I glare at him. "Are you saying that was Hannah?"

"I wasn't able to get a good look," he states and pushes himself up from where Devon was lying. "C'mon."

I stretch my fingers out and increase my fire. Flames lick vividly along the edges of my hand as we follow the uprooted trees. The ground still rumbles and groans as if it's ready to take on another soul. And then one by one, the sigils begin to glow. Each casts out a light connecting and weaving into a circle and blocks us from entering. In the center is the woman forcing Devon up from the clutches of the earth.

The woman squats down. Straggly, blonde hair disguises her face until she looks up. It's not Hannah. It's her mother, Catherine. She rises from her squatted position and releases the body with a thud. Evan decides to announce the obvious, "David, I think that's Hannah's mother…"

"I know," I mouth back.

Catherine tips her head to one side and then slowly to the other. Her features still hold that sweet, motherly look. "David? What are you doing out here?"

"We came to help Devon," I reply trying to keep my voice steady.

"Why? She's fine…see?" Catherine squats down again and lifts Devon up a bit. Her face is covered in dirt, her hair matted and disheveled. My heart pounds inside my chest, did she kill her dragging her below? But then, Devon suddenly sucks in a desperate gasp of air like she was submerged under water far too long. Catherine mumbles in a tender tone as she gently strokes Devon's cheek, "Scith, mo leanbh, tu uacht bheith marbh go luath." Catherine lays Devon back to the ground and stands.

Evan nudges me. "Her eyes." It's all he says, and I realize they're not sweet and benevolent-looking anymore. They're as black as an endless tomb.

"Don't fret. She still breathes," Catherine consoles, but not only has her eyes changed, but her voice also sounds deeper and demonic.

"What are you going to do with her?" Evan asks.

"Don't you know sacrifices have to be made," Catherine answers with a ruthless tone. She folds her hands in front of herself like a paragon of virtue from a strange religious order. Barefoot and dressed in solid white with elegant soft coils of blonde draping over her in the purest form. I'm having a hard time wrapping my head around the fact that a demon is controlling her.

"What about the witch's rede? As it harms none, do as thou wilt, lest in thy self-defense to be, ever mind the rule of three. Follow this with mind and heart. Merry ye meet, and merry ye part. Doesn't 'harm none' mean *anything* to you?" I ask.

Her body bends back as she laughs. It's not a normal laugh, it's hair-raising and sinister. She drops her head forward and leers at us with those black, sunken-in eyes. "I'm protecting our kind. You think when a full moon rises they refrain from harming us?" she says and points a long, crooked finger to Devon. "I'm protecting my girls." She moves a few feet closer; the reddish hue of light still guards the circle. "You could help protect the girls, David." Her tone distorts from diabolical to merciful, and for a split second, she looks like the motherly Catherine I know. "Join me. There's so much more we have to do."

"Let Devon go," Evan implores. "We know you only want to help your family, but this is not the way."

"This is the way I'm afraid. We must walk the path of the righteous. Give ourselves completely to the divine, and only then will we be favored by Namtar."

I glance over to Evan and whisper, "Who's Namtar?"

"The demon," he mumbles quietly.

Catherine hovers along the boundary. "I need to get back to Elijah, he's waiting to honor the ritual. Won't you join us?" she pleads with a guilt-free expression and then wheels around on her bare heels and ambles toward Devon. "I know you want to come inside," the demon speaks through her again. The deep, monstrous tone saturates the air like the gathering storm looming above. The night sky hums with a fierce resonating sound and every hair on the back of my neck rises. I know I should be worrying about how to get Devon the fuck out of here, but I can't help the dire need to find Hannah. As if the demon knows what I'm thinking, it contorts Catherine's body to the side. Bones crack unnaturally and a deformed smile hangs grotesquely from her lips. "You want to know where she is? Come inside the circle, David."

I start to move forward as the veil of the circle descends, but Evan immediately jerks me back. "Namtar is tempting you, David," he sharply cautions.

As Catherine's disjointed body turns toward us, she lifts an arm outward. "If you don't want to join me…then leave!" Her hands push forward, Evan and I are violently hurled backward. We have no control as if the demon drained us from our powers. We sail through the air like a bullet firing from a gun, and without any warning, collide into the trees.

Chapter Twenty-Four

Droplets of water trickle across my face, I groan and roll over to my side. An earthy smell drifts through my nose, and I open my eyes. Daylight glistens over the raindrops bouncing quickly from leaf to leaf. I blink trying to normalize my focus and examine the dense thicket surrounding me. Evan's a few feet away. He's knocked out cold. His body is slumped over against a fallen evergreen tree. A touch of red runs down his neck. I scramble to my feet and stagger to him.

"Evan…?" I call out, but he doesn't move. I stoop down and shake him. "Evan, damn it. Wake up!" His limp body sways as I relentlessly continue to shake him. "Evan!" He makes a low sound, and then he pries an eye slowly open. "Where's the demon?"

"I don't fucking know," I glance back and find nothing out of the ordinary. "I think it's gone. It probably took Devon somewhere," I reply and grab him with one arm. "Come on, easy, Ev." He rises up with me and rubs the back of his head.

"The demon's been feeding," he says, leaning some of his weight against me as we walk through the woods.

"What makes you say that?" I ask.

"It held too much power… and I think from what Catherine said, *there was more to do*. If it takes more souls, more bodily forms it can fully restore to its natural state of being."

"Sounds intriguing. I can't wait," I state sarcastically. As much as I hate it, Evan's right. If I had enough strength I could easily levitate Evan back to the hotel, but I'm lucky I can walk. The rain beats down on us drenching our clothes.

"I wonder what time it is?" Evan questions.

"I don't have a clue. I imagine your phone is probably dead, too?"

"Yeah." He wipes some of the blood off from his neck and glances at me. "Do you think Hannah's okay?"

"I'd know if there's something wrong with her. I guess that's the benefits of being bound," I remark. As we tread back into town I keep quiet trying to feel that lifemate connection. Trying to feel if she's in pain or suffering, but I'm not getting any vibe she's in trouble. Eventually, we make it to the hotel, and I scrub off first and grab some clean towels. Evan cleans up in the bathroom, and while he's in there I rub my hands together. My parents are healers and I have that ability to an extent. If I summon enough energy I might be able to mend Evan's wound.

"Hey, how are you feeling?" I ask as Evan pulls out a chair.

"I think I'm going to live, David."

I walk around him and see the gash where he hit the tree. "I'm going to try and heal that."

"No. You need to save your energy. I'm fine," he states dragging his hands down his worried face. "I think it's time we call in the Worthington's." He drops his hands to his knees and looks at me with frustration. "We know Catherine and Devon are gone. And seeing that demon…" he pauses shaking his head. "take on Catherine's form like it was nothing. David, this could very well be stronger than both of us."

"Do you believe Catherine took the tourists?

His grim silent nod tells me what I need to know and then he says, "Elijah could've been the one telling her to bring the sacrifices, but then last night, the demon possessed her."

"But I didn't see the book, did you?" I question pacing the floor.

He sighs heavily. "No."

"So, it's only a matter of time Namtar will take on his full form, right?"

"Correct," Evan remarks.

I make my way to the window and watch the rain pelt the narrow street below. In my journeys searching for the Brotherhood, I never crossed a demon alone. Jinn was my first to encounter and she wasn't anything like Namtar. She had no need to ravage the weak and manipulate to become stronger. She was only out for payback to those who had summoned her.

Namtar hungers for flesh, bones, and souls of the lost. My heart aches for Hannah when she finds out her mother is gone. Catherine was just following the orders from Elijah. Parts of her still echoed through the demon, *she wanted to protect her girls*. But instead, she opened up something none of us expected. The witches that had dabbled in the dark arts were a walk in the park for me. Yes, I deprived them of life because there was no turning back for them. I fought and hunted ruthlessly to keep a demon from awakening. But now, my worst fear has become a reality. A reality I'm not sure Evan and I can handle. I peer over my shoulder. "You're lookin' pretty rough, Ev. Why don't you take a quick shower and shave?" I stare back outside and watch the black umbrellas dot the drizzly, sunless scenery.

"David? You, all right?" Evan asks.

"Yeah," I state trying to keep my voice sounding neutral. "Thought I almost lost you back there."

"No. I'm invincible, remember?" he jokes.

"The invincible *Water man*. Sounds pretty fucking impressive if you ask me," I return. The shower turns on and my stomach grumbles reminding me it's time to eat. Maybe grabbing some food will help improve my mood. I check the time, and it's almost noon. "Hey, I'll be back in a few. I'm going to find a pizza or something," I yell out. Just as I reach for the doorknob a burning prickle runs down my spine. It's like a sixth sense because I have a brief flashing image of Hannah standing on the other side.

I swing the door open. "Are you okay?" I ask and yank her inside. I check the hallway making sure she wasn't followed. She's soaked to the bone. Her hair is thickly matted to her face as she pants, "I have it. David…I have the book."

"What?"

She rummages around inside a large tan shoulder bag and hands over a book. "See? I was able to get it this morning. Can you read it, because it looks cryptic? Maybe the words are just scrambled, you think?" she questions completely fixated. Her wet body brushes against mine as she flips through the pages. Gently, I wrap my arm around her and utilize my fire. The soft color of her shirt brightens as it dries, and from her skirt down to her sandals show no sign she was soaked by the rain. She pulls back her hair, touching the waterless curls, and smiles. "Thank you," she says and immediately looks back at the book in my hands.

The outside texture is coarse and uneven, leather-bound, and black. I run my hand over the high raised surfaces that look like roots swirling around one red eye. The thick pages are worn, but on each page are the same sigils that were in the woods last night. Designs of a half-man, half-beast with horns sprouting from his jaws hanging down to his clawed feet, appear on a few pages. I scan the symbols and the lettering, and none of it I can interpret. It's like looking at a damn jigsaw puzzle and some of the pieces are missing.

"The invocations are all there, the summoning of Namtar," Evan says over our shoulders. Hannah and I both glance over to him as he buttons his clean, crisp shirt. He looks more himself, but the gnawing concern is still there etched inside his dark eyes. "This book wasn't just created, it's old," Evan states as he glides a finger along the frayed pages.

Hannah taps on a peculiar, round symbol. "I've seen one of these out by our house. My father said it was for protection." She steps away and stares at Evan. "It was never for protection was it?"

"I'm afraid not, Hannah," he replies soberly.

"Look… I have to go," she quickly states standing by the door.

"Hannah, wait." I drag my hand nervously through my rumpled hair and debate with myself. *How am I going to tell her about her mother? How does anyone tell someone they lost a loved one? How do I tell her and not shatter her heart?*

"My father's probably leaving the café soon and I can't be gone when he figures out the book is not there, David." She pulls me close to her and gently kisses my lips. "I'm going to be fine. It's a full moon tonight. So, meet me later on the south side of the lake, okay?"

My mouth still hangs foolishly open as she closes the door. "I couldn't tell her, Evan."

He places a hand firmly on my shoulder and says, "There's going to be time to tell her, and you'll explain it at the right time. Now that we have the book, David. No more harm can be done."

Chapter Twenty-Five

I look in the mirror and try to manage my unruly hair. It looks like I just jumped out of bed and never thought twice about combing it. *Fuck it.* I toss the comb beside the sink and glare at Evan as he leans on the doorframe. "What?" I growl.

"You want me to go get the scissors?"

"I think I'll pass," I say striding by him. I grab another shirt out of my bag and change.

"You are worse than a woman, David. How many times are you going to swap out clothes?"

"Jeez, Ev," I mouth and hold up a navy-blue shirt. "Do you think this one matches my eyes better?" Evan laughs and turns away. "*All right*, I'll stop messing around. So… tonight, I'll find Hannah and you meet us back here and we hit the road, right?"

"That's the plan. Just be careful, David. I'm sure Elijah knows the book is missing."

"You have the book?" I ask.

"Yes. I have the book."

I sling my jacket on and snag my bike keys. "I'll be back at first light."

The streets are coated with a slick and glossy finish as the rain tapers off. My bomber bike rumbles mimicking the sound of thunder as I veer through the winding road eclipsed with a high green canopy of trees. The long stretch from the town to the lake becomes withdrawn just like the clouds abandoning the sky. My feelings are nothing but a jumbled-up mess. A need inside of me wants to protect Hannah, protect her from pain and heartache. It kills me to be the one to tell her about her mother, but I know this is something I will have to do. And the only thing I can do now is to make sure she's safe when the full moon unfolds.

Southbound, I catch the sight of the water. Rough and jagged waves beat savagely against a rocky overhang. A beacon of light shines above the cliff and a silhouette of a woman stands. It's a picturesque scene as she towers over the lake like a goddess controlling the waves. Each wave rhythmically curls into an arched form and breaks along the shoreline. Her powers are growing. I can sense the energy from her as I park my bike and navigate toward the overhang.

She's in a sheer, ivory dress and it fits her like how I imagined a deity of the earth would look – mystically stunning. She reaches a hand out as I approach. "Isn't it beautiful out here?"

I throw a quick look toward the vast open landscape and then stare at her. "Have you looked in the mirror?"

She looks over with a baffled expression, her light-colored brows pinch together as she asks, "No? Why? What's wrong?"

"Babe, you're more breathtaking than any of this," I state.

"So, you like the dress?"

"I love the dress. Although…I don't think it would fit me," I tease with a brash smile.

She chuckles softly and cups her hands around my face. "I love you, even when you're cocky."

"Cocky, huh?"

Her thin brow raises as she grins. "Do you know what else I love about you?"

"What's that?"

She presses her lips lightly against mine and tips her head, watching me. "The way you kiss me, and the way…" she pauses and slowly glides my hand over her hip. "The way you touch me." Her soft lips compel mine and we fall into a kiss that's unrushed and tender. My fire arouses, searing through every bone and vessel in my body. There's no need for a kerosene lamp out here because I'm like a damn blazing watchtower.

She moves just a teasing breath away, and says, "I love everything about you."

"You know, I've tried to avoid falling for someone for so long, that I thought love was a forsaken word, but now, I can't fight it. I won't fight it because there's nothing about you that would stop me from loving you."

"Even if I have no control over the change that's about to happen?" she asks.

"Yes. Even if you change into a wolf."

She softly pecks her lips along mine, and I can feel her smile.

I meet her kiss and then break away. "I'd still love you even if you turned into a toad."

Her smile widens. "Well, that's reassuring."

"I'd kiss you until I broke the curse," I say wandering my hands up, touching every curve of her body.

"And what if that toad wasn't me?" she asks.

I chuckle. "Well then, I would have to scrub all the slimy, toady-goo from my lips, make sure there's no traces of warts, and go toad hunting again until I found you."

"I think that's the most romantic thing I have ever heard, David."

I lift a shoulder and casually reply, "What can I say…I'm a guy in love."

A needling shiver races along my spine and I embrace Hannah instinctively. Silas peeks through the edges of the trees. I glare over to him. "I know you're there."

His pale, freckled face emerges out from the woods, his hands tucked inside his back pockets of his jeans. "You two look *really* cozy out here…" he draws out.

"Silas, were you just sneaking around in the woods? Shouldn't you be with the others?" Hannah asks.

"I could be askin' the same thing about you, Hannah," Silas remarks. He leans back and eyes the sky like he's trying to find some fine line between composure and pity. "It's sure is pretty out here. Don't you think, David?"

Tactfully, I move Hannah behind me. These are the times I'm thankful I have the levitation capability, there's no resistance. With my body guarding her I calmly reply, "Yeah."

"Funny how you work so damn hard for somethin' and then have an outsider just steal it right in front of your face," he states coldly.

"I'm going to go out on a limb here, and say, you're talking about me?" I reply.

He lowers his head and gawks around. "I don't see anyone else here, do you?"

"You got a problem with me, then show me what you got, Silas." I shift and meet him toe to toe.

He snarls at me grinding his teeth, "You're going to be the first flesh I taste tonight. But before I hunt you down like the piece of shit you are, I'm going after her," he swings his arm toward Hannah. As if on cue the full moon hovers against the cliffside. I watch as his facial features distort, eyes bulge, jaws elongate, skin twists and turns as a thick coat of reddish fur erupts. His teeth lengthen morphing into sharp, bone crushing fangs. Clothes suddenly flay outward as he charges at me. I release an armor of fire around myself. Silas shrilly yelps and quickly rectifies his attack. As sleek and swift as the blowing wind he bolts after Hannah and soars over the cliff.

Her severed dress dances across the soundless edge like a stranded phantom. I shift about thirty feet, striving to feel our bond. And then another thirty and get zilch. She's so far out that I can't track her. I swerve and make a hard right and head for my bike. A wolf howls as the moon climbs over the timbers, a low, indistinct noise rustles across the woods. My boot whips back the kickstand just as I spot the pack of wolves running through the tree-line. Silver-like fur streaks by just on the outskirts and an electrifying spark dictates my next move. It's Hannah. She lunges and crisscrosses whatever barrier that impedes her escape.

I flow through the gears keeping up with her, over fifty miles per hour we're hauling-ass through the serenading moonlight. She leads the pack like a conduit of strength. Fluid and graceful she wards off the impaling arrows that mount higher through the air. A true leader of the four-legged legion, she evades the next onslaught and scales the next craggily high-rising bluff. I lean into the following curve and feel claws drag down my arm before I see razor-like teeth viciously chomping at my face.

I jerk and let go of the clutch, my element surges, encasing my hand in flames. Silas' shapeshifted form clings to my jacket as he snaps ferociously at me. The residual water on the road undermines the bike's grip, and we skid sideways. I shift before my bike meets the asphalt. As my form rematerializes, an arrow suddenly sinks through my left shoulder jolting me backward. I grip the shaft and yank it out. Before I have my bearings to stumble forward, another wolf attacks. But not at me, I watch as snarling teeth with silvery grey fur collides into Silas. Hannah knocks Silas off his feet and strikes at his neck, it's nothing but a blinding entanglement of fur and fangs. Brutal growls arise between the two as each sink their teeth into bloodstained pelt and flesh. A sharp whimper releases from the maimed red wolf and he flees toward the woods.

The grey wolf only glances at me for a second like she's making sure I'm okay, and then hightails it in the same direction as Silas. I slip my hand under my shirt and feel the swell of my skin, the arrow didn't make it all the way through. But it still hurts like hell. My fingers press the lesion as a warmth accumulates within me and spreads like a wildfire healing and mending the damage. I let out a sigh, relieved that I had some energy to heal. The demon however he managed to do it sucked a lot of strength from me and Evan.

Fucking Namtar, he's like a walking magnet, pulling whatever power and strength he can once he's near you. I brush back the hair from my eyes and steady myself. Leah slows her jog toward me. Her coal-black mane hangs loose tonight, but she's leather clad and geared with the usual. A back quiver filled with arrows and a hunting knife tightly strapped to her thigh. "Which way did they go?" she asks scouting around.

I take a few steps out and pick up her arrow from the ground. "You might want to practice some more," I suggest handing it to her.

She reaches out with her left hand and I note the leather padded armguard. I wait for her to tell me it wasn't her, but she says, "Did I hit you?" She eases up on her tiptoes and closely examines my shoulder. "Huh," she pipes out indifferently and rubs a finger on my jacket, a dribble of blood still shows. Slowly, she rubs her two fingertips together. "Does it hurt?"

"Like a bitch," I reply.

She rocks back on her heels and smirks. "Well, then you just got a sample of what it will be like for every single wolf tonight because I'm going to slaughter all of them. They did something to Devon. *Yeah…*" she says glaring over her shoulder. "They took her, and you want to know how I know this? Simple. Every time something bad happens you can always point the finger at the Wolfenstein's. Devon never showed up this evening, and that's not like her."

"And you think hunting wolves down will…?" I ask pausing for a reasonable answer.

"Bring her back? Maybe, maybe not, but there's something we believe in, David. My people were taught that we all have our own battles inside, one part is struggling with arrogance, greed, false pride, lies and the other part is truth, love, peace, and generosity. The one that you feed will be the one that will win. And the Wolfenstein's, namely that old coot, Elijah, has desecrated this area with something unnatural and it has to be stopped." she says and wheels around throwing her arm up in the air. "I'm comin' for you! You hear me?! I'm coming to kill you all!"

As she faces away I have the chance to evoke a spell. I skim a fingertip over a fletching and vanquish every arrow in her leather quiver. It's a straightforward spell but how long it will hold, I'm not sure. Leah whips back around and brags, "Normally I never miss my target. You were just in my way, so count yourself lucky it wasn't a kill shot." She pokes at my chest and dashes off. Her Nakoa tribe, Jansen, Malcolm, Greg, and several others gather at the deer path leading deeper into the pines. If I shift fast enough I could wipe out all their weapons but the need to locate Hannah becomes my first priority.

I rationalize the reasons why Leah has a deep-seated hatred for the Wolfensteins. Witches agreeing to a pact, only to lead to a legacy of death and betrayal. It all just adds fuel to the fire, and she's seeing it in her own interpretation. This is why our kind typically keeps it low-keyed. *Fuck*, I mutter under my breath. This is not how I thought things would go. I lift my bike from the ground, start it up, and let it rumble while I try to grasp Hannah's connection.

With her being in a wolf form it's making it tricky to detect the lifemate pull. Maybe it's the demon's blood surging through their veins or the pack is restricting the vital link between us. I don't know, but I have to find her. The overland becomes pitted and rugged, each mile feels longer than the last, and then I get a glimpse of a large, black wolf. His sheen fur gleams in the wavering moonlight. His shape barrels through the groves covered with underbrush, he's bigger than any of the other wolves I've seen. Broad-shouldered, burly, and spry enough that he makes the overgrown woods look like a cinch. Before he swerves away, he stares me down with gory, pitch-black eyes.

It's Hannah's father, Elijah, and everything about him reeks with the demon's scent. I cut a hard right and fly down the next path. A tingling digs in my reflexes as if my subconscious rules my direction and I abruptly do a one-eighty. A streak of grey flashes in and out of the prickly brier and thistle sage. I watch quietly as she prowls close to the embankment beside the path, longing, steel-grey eyes search me. She's tired of running, tired of being chased down like a diseased creature. I peer up to the moon. "Just a few more hours before the sun rises," I say dropping my gaze to her. "I'm right here with you. We can do this, okay?"

She steps farther out, and I see that her paws and legs are splattered with sediment and sludge. Her lips curl back and a row of long, pointed flesh-tearing teeth bare. A low throaty growl releases, and then a sudden shriek slices through the dark. The Nakoa's call out, a piercing whistle drifts from one tree to the next. A high-pitched screech echoes back and I realize she wasn't growling at me; she's warning me that danger is nearby. A smooth silver-tipped arrow whizzes past us just missing Hannah by an inch. She hunkers down and leaps upward like a streak of lightning racing through the underwood. Driving the Nakoa's away from me, I rev my bike and let my flames unleash.

A wolf howls and the area is consumed by the sound of scampering feet plummeting to the ground. Their desperation to slaughter haunts the woods like a bloodthirsty war. Arrows navigate smoothly, drifting over branches, leaves, and limbs. A cry from a wolf rings throughout, and the entire essence of the woods stills. And then another wave comes in, fine-tipped and deadly, the arrows swoop and weave leaving only blood and tears. I cast out fire, scorching the feather lined projectiles as fast as I can. One hand on the bike, the other is sheathed in red-hot flames. The Nakoa's sly croons and whistles carry out with a steadfast tone. And it's harder to tell which path the next assault will come from.

I maintain some distance from Hannah allowing the bond to control my actions. If the fire swells inside I know it's time to set it free and incinerate whatever flies through the air. We avoid one raid by skirting the road and down a jagged incline toward the lake. She runs alongside me as the moon begins to sink to the west. Her body is beautifully sleek and strong as she lunges over waterlogged branches near the embankment. Her movements are fluid and precise cutting through the crevices up another stony ridge. My bike loses traction against the slippery slope and I quickly ditch it. I chase after her until we find refuge in a cave hidden along the cliffside.

She paces back and forth, panting. Her wolf instincts are still in fight or flight mode, but everything in me wants to touch her and make sure she's unharmed. I don't know who I'm fooling because I'm still on guard myself. I walk just outside the mouth of the cave and examine our surroundings. The lake serenades a lulling pattern, and I can't hear a whistle shrill out or the rustle of footsteps nearby. I stand protecting her, and gradually watch as the sun climbs the sky, and claims it for its own. It's unsettling the see the scenery change so radically, moments ago we were swallowed in darkness, while menace stalked her like she was fair game. Now, the sunrise paints an entirely different picture it's completely silent and serene.

I pivot around and shift back inside. Hannah's naked and cold to the touch. She cradles her body shivering. "Here," I offer slipping off my jacket. Beads of sweat glisten across her forehead. I ease my body next to her and hug her close. "I think they're gone."

"They usually are," she whispers with a slight shiver.

"What can I do?" I ask.

"Warm me up."

Gently I glide my heated hand along her arms and down her side, flames flicker and dance as if the element takes pleasure warming her. Hannah rolls over, facing me. "They took out more of us tonight than they ever have before," she whispers softly.

"And this is what it's like for you every full moon?"

She sighs like it pains her to admit it. "Every full moon."

"Hannah? We're leaving and I'm taking you with me," I announce.

Weakened from the transmogrification from wolf to witch she tries to stand. Droplets of perspiration trickle between her breasts, her long, lush hair forms into loops and curls. Her pupils in the center of her eyes contract and the night vision recedes. The last traces of the wolf finally fade. Quickly, I remove my t-shirt, and cover her body. It's long enough to not expose too much. I grab my jacket, throw it on and start to pick her up, but she stops me.

"David…I can't. What about my family?"

"We'll figure it out on our way into town. Right now, we need to leave," I state.

"I have to check on my sisters. Please understand I can't just leave without making sure they're all right."

"Okay then, I'll go with you," I remark and quickly gesture for us to head outside.

"No," she says and places her hands on my chest. "I have to find them, it's my responsibility, not yours, David. I don't think you understand, but I'm stronger because of our bond. I had none of the tonics or elixirs my father made last night. I could feel you as if you were standing right next to me. Like right now…. Please trust me and I promise I'll bring Chloe and Jess to the hotel. All right?"

Her eyes plead as she grips me tighter. Her thoughts and emotions bleed into me, she wants to protect them as much as I want to protect her. An air of confidence hangs on her every breath. I bite my tongue and force out, "*All right*, but if you're not at the hotel within the hour I will find you."

Her motions are so fast that it takes me by surprise as she shifts toward the entrance. "I will find them, I always have," she says providing a small smile.

Her smile doesn't help my growing fear, but she's agreed to leave and that sways me from arguing with her. "Hannah…"

"I know…I feel it," she says placing a hand over her heart. Our bond goes beyond the secret kiss behind a set of bleachers. It's physical and deep just like the way her blood completes the witch's mark on my arm, embedded and part of me. Her doubts are my doubts, her pain is my pain, and her ecstasy is my ecstasy. Ultimately, I have found the feelings that Dawson and Marc have with their own lifemates. It's no longer just me, it expands further than my wildest imagination. And when I see that look in her eyes, the need to protect someone she loves, I get it.

We separate, she heads to the lake house and I travel back into town. Mistcove has an inexplicable reality. Shops open for business. Freshly baked foods are carried in and everyone seems blind to the carnage that took place in the backwoods. The only witness was the full moon and I'm guessing the majority like it that way. I ride through the peart little town as the windows are cleaned, sidewalks are swept, and smiles spread like an epidemic. It's just another lucrative day for them. I park and almost run smack-dab into an old woman. It's the same snowy-white haired woman with the floral purse.

"Excuse me, dearie," she says politely.

"No, I'm sorry," I quickly remark and start to maneuver around her.

"Could you pick that up for me? These bones of mine are as brittle as glass these days, and this here weather…" She wags a crinkly, small finger up at the sky. "can stir up the arthritis sometimes too."

"Sure thing," I reply and pick up the shiny object from the pavement. I recognize it immediately, it's a ring like the kind they sell at Quicksilver Jewels and Gems. I offer it to the old lady. "Here you go."

Her face scrunches up like I'm handing her a basket full of poisonous snakes and quickly draws away from me. "I can't touch that, but my intuition was right about you," she says clutching her purse.

I tip my head to the side curious and ask, "Why can't you touch it? It's yours isn't it?"

"Oh, honey, you should know by now I'm part of the Willowshire coven. I own this hotel." She leans back and stares at the tall, prehistoric-looking building with great pride.

I'm not sure what she wants me to say. So, I mumble out with, "*Ah*... okay."

She turns back with a kind smile. "Hope you and your friend have enjoyed your stay."

I try to hide my shock. *How did she know we were leaving?*

"Yeah, everything was great," I calmly state.

She chuckles. "Oh honey, no one ever stays for too long in Mistcove. People *always* come and go. It's just us that are cursed to stay in this wretched place, but enough of that. You boys be safe on your journeys." She ambles away toting her fancy, flowered handbag. Suddenly, I look around and find I'm the only one standing in the empty parking lot. I shake off the questions that are forming inside my mind and head for the room.

Chapter Twenty-Six

"I think I know why this place feels so damn creepy," I remark to Evan while I rifle through my stuff.

"Why is that?" he asks neatly folding a pair of slacks in a beige swanky suitcase.

"I bumped into the owner of this place. You know the one that carried the flowery purse we met in the elevator?

He squints a look in my direction like he's trying to remember. "I think so."

"She's got all those tacky photographs hanging on the walls… the ones that have eyes following you?" I state tugging a shirt on.

"I never felt like they were following me, but *okay*," he remarks.

"She mentioned something about us leaving. I think she's been doing her own undercover work here at the hotel." I look behind a picture hanging on the wall of our room and then glare over to Evan.

He zips his bag and replies with a decisive look. "Would it put your mind at ease if I told you that I have us listed for *checking-out* today by noon?"

I cram my laundry bag inside another duffle bag and scowl. "Nice, thanks for letting me think I was under surveillance by the geriatric council."

Evan glances at his phone. "Ah… David? Shouldn't Hannah be here by now?"

It's been two hours since we left the shore of the lake. I figured it would take Jess and Chloe some time to absorb everything that's happened. Especially when Hannah tells them about the book and the danger it possesses. Evan gives a brief visual inspection of the bathroom making sure we're not leaving anything behind. While I'm scanning beneath the beds a sudden light tap raps on the door. "That's probably her," I say jumping to my feet, but Evan beats me there.

He cracks the door open. "Gemma, what are you doing here?"

Her voice is barely a whisper as she says, "Is Hannah here?" Evan opens the door farther and motions for her to come inside. "I can't find Grandmother Greta or Catherine. I thought maybe Hannah would know but…"

"She's not here," Evan quickly states. Gemma starts massaging the side of her temple as she slumps down in one of the brown wingback chairs. Her strong features are highlighted with worry. I levitate another chair closer and Evan takes the hint and sits alongside her. "What's going on, Gemma?"

"Last night was intense," she says leaning back. "We had the ritual last night like Elijah usually does it, but he was acting off-the-wall. I mean, he restricted the elixirs to hardly nothing and stashed the rest for himself. It was really weird because normally he was very adamant about us drinking every last drop before we changed. Not this time. And on top of all this, I don't remember seeing my sister there at all." She stares over to me pensively, and then lets out a pent-up sigh. "There's a lot of our coven missing this morning, I'm afraid something's happened."

Evan leans forward with his elbows on his knees listening intently. I walk by Evan and wonder if we should tell her about the book. "All right you two… you know something," Gemma straightens her back and aims a finger toward me. "What is it?"

Evan cups his hands together and lowers his head. "Gemma…Your sister is gone. Elijah has a book that summons a demon. And this demon has taken Catherine's soul, her body, I mean everything. She's gone… *I'm sorry—*"

"No…it's not true. She would have never let Elijah do that to her," Gemma rebukes with tears swelling in her blue eyes. She lifts herself from the chair, brushes away a teardrop rolling down her cheek. "I knew things were starting to get bad out there, but I never thought Elijah would go this far, that fucking bastard." Her hands clench into fists as she paces like a caged animal. She spins around on her heels and says, "We have to find them." Fear and desperation cling to her words.

"Hannah was supposed to meet us here over an hour ago," I remark picking up a bag. "We'll head out and start searching."

Gemma reaches for Evan as he stands. Her eyes study his with a flood of emotions, but she quickly refrains herself from getting too emotional. "If Grandmother Greta is safe then she'll know where the girls are. Most of the elders here have hideouts, a place that's sheltered and magically protected. It's a bitch to find but that's where I'm going to first, okay?"

Evan flashes an uneasy look at me but before he voices his thoughts, a loud knock drums at the door. "I bet that's Hannah," I announce.

I swing it open and come face-to-face with the Brotherhood.

Two witches wearing black three-piece suits with long overcoats, their eyes match their ties, dark as a raven's wing. One's a hair inch taller than the other, but both have groomed, precisely trimmed crew-cuts. They appear to be a few years older than Evan and me, each with a slender build, and sinister looking stance. I stare at them and they stare back at me, and then finally the taller one speaks, "I believe you have something that belongs to us."

I'm still white-knuckling the door and peer around. A dash of a freckled face guy with tousled red hair hovers just behind them. "Yeah?" I bluntly reply.

"We would like it back," the shorter witch states.

Silas bobs his head between them grinning from ear to ear. "She brought you the book…" he blathers glaring me down. "Now you're gonna pay. Tell him, Darick." Silas jeers and smiles as he switches his glance toward Darick and the other Brotherhood member.

"Why you *fucking little*—" I start to mouth but Evan cuts in.

"You're not getting the book back," Evan counters pushing me away.

"Is that so?" the shorter one asks with a pleased look on his domineering face. A tiny curve like a creeping smile drifts over his lips. He cranes his head toward his partner and even from behind Evan, I can see the glistening anticipation in his black soulless eyes.

Darick's posture is reserved and stoic with his hands threaded together in front of his long coat. "I think we can be civil here. You have something that is of no use to you…it would be wise to give it back."

Evan shakes his head. "You're not getting the book back."

"Very well then, have it your way, Evan. Hannah is of no use to us. So, I hope you will have no grievance when she dies. Unless of course, you are willing to reevaluate your decision?"

Silas' mouth gapes open as he jerks on the two Brotherhoods. "What?! You said she wouldn't be harmed!"

Chaos erupts as Silas yells demanding answers, and I'm trying to break free from Evan's grasp. "You better not touch her!" I struggle against him feeling the flames soak through my flesh. "You hear me?! I'll make you wish you were facing that demon of yours instead of me!"

Darick whispers something over to Silas like he's simply telling him the time and then suddenly Silas' mouth vanishes. Nothing but freckled skin. Silas frantically starts patting at his mouthless face, mumbling ensues as his eyes widen in shock. I take a step back as Evan moves forward.

"I know your games, Darick. How do I know she's not already dead?" Evan asks.

"I do believe your friend there, already knows the answer. Don't you, David? Lifemates can be such a remarkable thing don't you think? One more reason for you to meet us at the old house tonight. Bring the book and we'll bring the girl." Darick swoops an arm over Silas, tendrils of darkness swarm around them like smoke twisting together, and then all three are gone.

Chapter Twenty-Seven

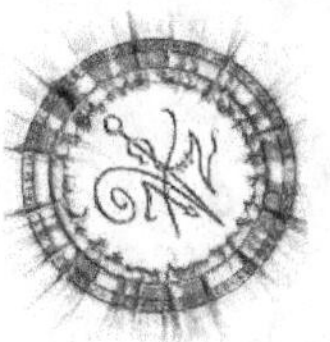

Gemma flips one of the drapes back and scans around outside. "I think they've left." She looks at us with a hand on her hip and questions, "Who are those guys?"

"The Brotherhood, well two of them anyway," Evan replies shoving the rest of our things in duffle bags.

"Why was Silas with them like he's some sort of lackey?" she inquires again helping Evan pack up.

"He's the one that met with the Brotherhood and got the book from them. Apparently, Silas had this bright idea Elijah would do a trade, a demon's book for Hannah. But now we have the demon's book, and they have Hannah," Evan hastily explains the condensed version and hands me a luggage bag. "Here, take this to the car, David. After tonight there shouldn't be any traces of us here."

"I'm not waiting around for tonight, Ev. I'm going to that fucking house right now," I remark dropping the bag by the door.

"David, listen to me. You cannot go out there now and not alone. It could be more than just the two of them. The Brotherhood are always scheming. How do you think Silas even got the book? He just walked up one day and said, *oh, nice book. Mind if I have it?* No… the Brotherhood had this all planned. They're always preying on the weak and if they find that soft spot on you then they will use it. It's a never-ending cycle for them because this is their way of life."

Gemma pulls her flowy red hair up in a tight bun and grips Evan's arm. "What do you need me to do? I'll go with you to the house, but first I have to find Chloe and Jess. Grandmother Greta has enough smarts to get the hell out of here when she knows it's time."

Evan glances back at me. "We'll help Gemma look for them, and then *we* will get Hannah back, David. All right?"

I let go of the doorknob and grudgingly nod.

———

Once we have everything in his car, we scour the remote areas. Houses become sparse, a few peek through the countryside but the farther out we go the fewer they become. My nerves are unraveling, and I can't stop the distressing feeling burning me up inside. *Is she safe?* Those words thrash around, and I can't seem to focus. *Am I just sensing my own agitation or is it hers?*

I lean my head against the backseat and drag my hands over my face. *Fuck!*

"David," Evan says from the driver's seat. His eyes watching me from the rearview mirror. "The Brotherhood could have some kind of spell cloaking her from you. Just try and relax."

"Relax? I can't fucking relax," I retort and roll down the window. The wind whips at my face as I take in the terrain. Rickety, battered signs dangle from rusty nails, they're lopsided but readable, Bard Passage, Cavern Road, Gray Way, and the Willows Path. It's a crossroads. Gemma lightly taps the dash. "Stop," she demands and hops out of the car, leaving the passenger door wide open. Each dirt road looks the same and as the wind blows against the slats of warped wood the signs flip in a different direction. I scratch the side of my jaw and stare at Evan. "How are we supposed to know which way to go if the signs keep moving?" I ask.

Evan gets out of the car and says, "There's only one way to find out, c'mon."

Gemma bends down, her jeans settle against the soft turf as dust cradles around her. She centers herself and draws a circle. She spreads her hands out and places them on the ground, the circle radiates with energy. Her thumbs touch, along with her index fingers forming a triangle in the sacred space and then enounces a spell, "I call upon the Source of all things to instill within me the wisdom of foresight, through which, I may harm no one. I call upon my familiarity and manifest my desire to know, dare, will, and keep silent." The soil beneath her hands move as if she were awakening a sleeping child. Sluggishly turning and tossing, but Gemma doesn't grow impatient. She chants the spell again, repeating each word with an alluring tone, beckoning for her enchantment to be heard. Again, the tiresome clay, rocks, and dirt churn with slumber but then a small coal colored stone unearths itself.

In the heart of her triangular area, the stone flits to the left and then to the right as if it can't make up its mind. "That's it…show me the way," Gemma coaches the stone. It spins around charged with life and rises a notch above her hands. The wedge-shaped end points toward the Gray Way. She picks it up, kisses it, and quickly says, "Thank you." Rising from the ground, she dusts off her blue jeans and tugs on Evan's hand. "Come on…that's where Grandmother Greta is at, and hopefully, the girls are with her."

I ride in the backseat watching how the view reforms. The sycamores, blue oaks, and willows unveil a road that looks long forgotten. A sound like someone sitting in an old rocking chair resonates throughout as the trees bend and bow allowing us permission to travel through. We pass by a pasture filled with ryegrass and cattails and then up a hill. Away from everything sits a stone pile, a cairn. Different shaped rocks stacked scantily one on top of the other, but as a flurry of wind rushes past, the stone pile never stirs. "Here, this is it," Gemma comments and pulls out a small velvet pouch. Evan parks alongside the grassy pastureland and we get out. As Gemma separates the raw gemstones she looks over to me. "You ready for this?"

I quirk a brow upward and ask, "For?"

She squares her shoulders and lowers herself in front of the tower of rocks. "For our family, the curse drains our magick, our elements when we change. I've tried to restore some of my magick, but it's not an easy task, and I'm going to need some help, okay?" She plucks a bloodstone from her palm, rolls it between her fingertips, and whispers softly, "I am Gemma born of power, goodwill, and wisdom. Though born of this world, my race is of the stars and moon. With harm to none, I manifest my will. To know, to dare, to will, and to be silent."

The gentle breeze swirls against her face, wine-red strands flutter along her cheeks like a ghost playfully toying with her hair. But then nothing happens, and the air becomes static. Gemma quickly takes out another gem. It's rough, not smooth like the others, basic looking like an ordinary rock. A lodestone. She clutches it with one hand and says, "This one here has a magnetic force. It will draw our powers together and we can see what is hidden beyond the greensward." She motions for Evan to come closer and places her hand in his. "Call upon your element. David, I need you to do the same, and together, we can free the illusion."

I carefully rest my right hand over theirs, embracing the relic-like stone. Water pools between my fingers, vines sprout along my hand, and fire intermingles with the elements. Each merging and unmerging until they are united and shape into a sphere of power. Gemma recites her invocation composedly. Her eyes closed; her lips barely move but I can feel the strength of our intent. One by one, a twine from the illusion spell falls away like pruning a lilac bush. I glance over and see a house fading in and out. Tall reeds and the long-stemmed grass gently sway with the wind as my fire dwindles out, and I move away. Evan stares over to Gemma. "You think the girls are there?"

Gemma slips her gems back inside the pouch and replies, "Yeah, I do. There's only one other witch that knows a spell like that…Grandmother Greta." She tucks the pouch in her back pocket, and we make our way toward the house. Ten feet away from the porch Chloe races down the steps. "Gemma! David!" she yells and slams into Gemma nearly knocking her off her feet. "We tried to get Hannah out of the house! But…they…" Chloe cries. Her entire demeanor is rife with fear. "Silas *t-told* them about a book and *he-e*…" she stammers out, tears slide down her face. "Brought those men, *those witches* to our house—"

Jess appears beside us and says, "They did something to our mother and if it weren't for Grandmother Greta I don't know where we'd be. She took us through the underground tunnels, you know the ones, Aunt Gemma?"

Gemma hugs the girls tight in her arms. "I'm so sorry this happened. We're going to find your sister," she states.

Grandmother Greta treads the path toward us. "Elijah is with them, David. He is buried so deep in this black magick, that I don't think the Goddess can even save him now," she says gently patting my arm. "I see your pain and I feel it too, but you need to remember as long as you feel this…" She places her small delicate hand over my chest and says, "then you know she's still among us and you have to save her from those that are bound in darkness."

Chapter Twenty-Eight

"I'm going to help Evan and David," Gemma says, kissing Jess and Chloe on their foreheads. "You're safe now."

Evan eases over to her, his eyes make contact with hers as he advises, "I think it's better if you stay here, Gemma. You can help protect them, together you'll be stronger. The Brotherhood are bloodthirsty and will sacrifice as many as they can, humans, nonhumans, witches, whatever they can to gain the power from the summoned demon. I should know, I was one of them."

"What? *But*…you're not like them," Gemma replies. A fearful look edges around her confused expression.

"No. I'm not like that anymore," he confesses and shoots a brief glance at me. "I had help, and I was able to walk away from the wrath of the Brotherhood." He briefly touches her cheek and then shifts to the car.

Gemma turns, sadness and despair taint her voice as she asks, "David?"

"We're going to get Hannah," I state with resolve and follow the path back. Grandmother Greta, the girls, Gemma, and the house all wither into the background. It's nothing but a surplus of spacious hidden land and no one would be any the wiser. As soon as I shut the passenger's door, Evan high-tails it. We speed through the crossroads and navigate the secrets that would perplex most. Each direction could possibly lure you to a closed-off passage, restricting you from making any progress. But since Gemma showed us the way it doesn't take long to get to the lake.

The driveway to the main house comes into view. The air is stiff and laden with their presence. Evan turns the engine off as we sit inside the car taking stock of what we see and don't see. The screen door scarcely hangs on a hinge. Inside is a soft wavering light that shines like it's an omen and I can already sense the vileness that's taken over. A heavy haze rises from the east and layers over the waters, sweeping, pulsating a shadow of murk. The outer edges of the Wolfenstein's property are concealed by woods, but Evan and I both know the timbers are not the only thing flanking the house.

Evan removes a pocket-sized satchel similar to the one Gemma had and withdraws a strand of hair that is golden and long. He holds it in his hand and says, "I'm gonna need a little assistance tracking her, David. I'm not bound to her and this will help."

"Where'd you get that?" I ask.

"Gemma gave it to me before we left. Now singe the ends," he states and hands it over to me. I swallow down the blistering blaze that lurks up my throat. The fine silky thread falls against my palm and I nearly come unglued. Flashes of panic, anguish, and dread smother my own emotions. These are her emotions. I quickly grasp one end and scorch the tip and do the same to the other. Evan quickly takes it and ties it into a knot. He chants a spell that's as old as time and folds the strand inside a torn piece of cloth. "This should do, but like I said earlier, they could have their own spell reversal or simply have her cloaked from us."

"Yeah," I grumble and get out of the car. Discussions, plotting, negotiations— I've decided I'm pretty much done with it because I'm out for blood. My body shakes like an inferno that just consumed every fiber of my being.

"David…David?!" Evan raises his voice chasing after me. "You're not going in there and burn everything to a crisp. All right? Hey…would you stop for a second?" Evan shifts in front of me and blocks my way inside.

"Move, Evan," I sternly order.

"Kill the flames or you're going to set the porch on fire," he demands and cuts a threatening glare at me. "*Or* you can go inside looking like you just took a dip in the lake." Water vapors suspend around him and accumulate between us. And then in a blink, his hand swivels outward drenching my arms. The flames that coated along me just seconds ago hiss and seethe like a storm sucking the life out of a wildfire. He's made his point, but I can rekindle the fire just as fast as he can form a torrent of rain.

"What are you two doin' out here? Havin' a pissin' match?" Elroy asks popping his head out of the doorway.

Evan steps back and eyes Elroy. I sidestep around them and enter the house. "Evan, this is Elroy, the girls' uncle. Elroy this is Evan. Now that we're done with the pleasantries, where's the Brotherhood bastards?"

Elroy limps over and picks up a broken chair. "They're not here. They took off after Elijah. I'm supposin' he thought he would get off scot-free and unscathed by all this devilry."

Evan snags a glass rolling around on the floor and sniffs it. "Were you drinking this?" he asks Elroy.

"Do I look like I'm deranged?" Elroy snaps and plops down on the couch rubbing the blood off the side of his face. "I came over here as soon as I started hearing the ruckus. I saw what they did to Catherine. Why Elijah let'em sacrifice her like that I have no idea and he just stood there like a bump on a damn log."

I kick shards of glass away with my boot and kneel in front of Elroy. "And what the fuck did you do while they took Hannah?"

Elroy grits his teeth and scoots to the edge of the couch. "Boy, there wasn't much for any of us to do after the full moon. Don't you know the change drains us? We're lucky we can conjure a stick, but you bet your ass I damn sure tried to fight'em off."

I turn my aggravated gaze away from him and look around. Potted plants lay smashed and scattered, handsewn curtains sag feebly on bent rods. Most of the detailed hand-crafted furniture, whether it had been Elijah's work or fashioned with magick, rests in ruins. Everything is mangled and tossed around as if it were useless garbage.

"How did you escape them, Elroy?" Evan asks roaming by us. He picks up a tattered book, loose pages swish back and forth, and land beside his sorrel shoes.

Elroy grunts with a grim face. "*Escape?* You mean how did I slip through their fingers? I didn't… I played dead."

I shoot a suspicious squint toward him and ask, "You what?"

"What are you deaf? I said, I played dead…" he shakes his head like he's cross with us but adds, "That one tall fella was dragging Hannah out of the house and that other scoundrel…" he snaps his fingers a few times and then lifts a gouged, bloody brow. "Louis, that's his damn name. Came at me swinging one fist after another like I was some kind of punching bag. I got a couple of good hits in, but it didn't seem like it fazed him in the slightest. He just laughed and threw me over the table. After that he never laid another hand on me…'cause his element was too busy thrashing and beating me around. I flew into the wall and it nearly knocked me out. So that's when I figured to play it out and act like I was as dead as a doornail. I heard him walk over to me, but as soon as that other snake in the grass hollered his name he was gone."

Evan rummages through the drawers in the kitchen and comes back with a damp cloth. "Here, clean yourself up. Darick and Louis have been with the Brotherhood for some time now. They've been on demon's blood enough to amp-up their powers. I'm surprised though…why they didn't take you?"

Elroy swipes the cloth along his busted mouth and grumbles, "You think I'm worth anything to them? Shit no." He waves a hand over himself, ragged, worn, and barely has enough strength to stand— *let alone walk.* "No, boys, I have seen too much of this. They want fresh meat to feed that demon Elijah always talked about. He'd thought the Gods and Goddesses favored him more the day Silas brought him that book. The work of the true righteous will bestow upon them the promise of everlasting power." He grunts with disgust. "I bet my brother now sees the *everlasting power,* but it's not him that reaps the benefits. Now is it?" He cuts a bleak look toward us. And then he brushes by cradling the right side of his ribs and hobbles down the hall. "Elijah had this one trap door here," he says bending down and tosses a handstitched rug over. "To take him wherever he wanted. Tunnels that lead to other shafts underground, most are barricaded with a number of spells. With any luck, David. You might be able to figure out which way they took Hannah."

As Evan pulls the wooden hatch open, I climb down the long and narrow ladder. Wrought iron lamps hang from chains casting out a ray of light. Evan stands beside me. "I told Elroy to hang back and guard the house."

"Guard? *Guard what?* The couch and the one oil lantern in the house?" I shrug him off and head toward the first stone archway I see. Dampness and the scent of decay have a death-grip on the atmosphere. The deeper we go the tighter the air feels like a noose, tense and drawn, ready to choke the last breath out of you. As I skim around a corner I hear faint voices. The words ripple and wander as if they're taunting me to change my direction. Evan has my back as I continue to move forward. "Looks like someone's been doing some finger painting," I remark in a low voice and point at the runes along the walls.

"Yeah, in blood," Evan dryly replies.

We take the next passage. Six barriers line the corridor, and all are enshrouded with an irradiance of spell work. There's an intense power locked and weaved inside each that spreads through the thick cross-grained walls. Boulder stones and a maze of magick keep anyone from entering, and then the tiniest waver of our bond hits me. My fire unfurls and I know Hannah's in here somewhere. Evan abruptly drops the strand of hair. As it falls it untwines itself from the knot he had made and lands with a wispy curl. He immediately looks at me, silently I nod and slink up to the first barrier. I carefully place my hands along the pulsating energy. It beats and hums as if it were a living, throbbing heart. It's incessant and strong. Before I'm able to utter a word to untangle Elijah's casting a voice says, "What are you doin' down here? The party is up there…" Silas jabs a thumb over his shoulder and grins. Out of thin air, Louis takes shape and stands beside him.

"Yeah, David. Don't you want to throw a few cold ones back and enjoy tonight, *although*…" Louis says, and then a rush of air swooshes around and forces us to move forward. Evan and I are a mere foot away from Silas and Louis. "You are a little early but that's fine we can always use some help setting things up for the ritual."

Chapter Twenty-Nine

Louis slings back his long overcoat and drapes an arm over Evan. "I bet you miss that rich, savory taste. It's like a fine wine, but *oh*, it gets even better after that. Doesn't it Evan? Your veins pop with potency and the stronger the demon, the stronger you feel. You miss it, don't you?" Louis questions squeezing Evan's shoulders.

Evan grips Louis' arm and jerks it away. "You sound like Nate, foolish, and pretentious."

"Oh man, those were the days. You may think Nate was unwise, but he did stir up some hell, didn't he?" Louis reminisces.

"He's dead now, in case you forgot," Evan remarks.

Louis shrugs like it's of little consequence to him and stuffs his hand inside a pocket of his dress slacks. His eyes glisten in black, no hint of any other color much like his attire— showy and dark.

"I see you have your mouth back, Silas," I quip.

Silas narrows his eyes at me while I walk around him. "You better watch yourself, David. I might just do the same to you since I have this demon's blood in me."

"Is that so?" I ask leaning closer. He slants back away from me and every muscle in his face twitches like he's ready to take me on.

"Well as much as I enjoy this damp, dreary tunnel, I think it's time to get this party started. What do you say, Silas?" Louis questions with a subtle smirk.

Silas' shifty dark eyes bounce between me and Louis. "*Yeah*, let's get this started."

Evan keeps his pace with me as we trudge through the whispering corridors. Wind accompanies us, pushing against our backs making sure we don't lag too far behind. We breach a section with a wooden ladder and light trickles in. I climb up and Evan mumbles, "We're at the building Leah showed me."

"You mean the one you showed me a picture of?" I ask glancing at the gutted-out structure. Enormous oak posts support the underbelly of the floor above. Ink-carved candles and tarnished oil lamps form a ring in the center. A few dust covered chairs sit randomly to the side, the windows are covered with sheets and I quickly get the impression this is their sacrificing grounds.

"Yes." Evan eases over and states, "They call it the witch's house."

"Fitting, I guess if you're thinking of an old hag that likes to eat little children and brews up eye of newt," I retort and follow Silas and Louis. Unusual symbols, whittled into posts, brighten as I pass. It's a trajectory of light filled with sorcery, beaming from one end to the other. Louis kicks a chair my way. "Have a seat," he says and nudges Silas. "Make yourself useful and drag another chair over here."

"I'd rather stand," Evan evenly remarks, revealing nothing in his expression, but quietly he's observing everything around us and rightfully so. Dried splotches of blood tinge the floor like a high resin gloss. A thick chain swings from pillar to post waiting for its next victim. Silas lugs a chair over and slams it down beside me. Darick saunters in, with his cocky stride, and his fitted suit and oxford laced boots. He reminds me of a gang member from the 1920s.

Darick flips back his red-lined overcoat and pulls out a vial. Thick red liquid rolls gradually around as he moves it in-between his fingers. "Looks like we don't have enough for everyone. That's too bad," he says.

"Where's Hannah?" I ask knocking the chair out of my way.

"Where's the book?" Darick returns and calmly slips the vial inside his coat.

"We have it, but first we need reassurance she's unharmed," Evan demands, his whole stature remains rigid and sharp.

Darick straightens his tie and motions at Silas. "Bring the girl."

Silas' floppy red hair bobs up and down as he dashes off. He heads below and into the shadowy tunnels. "We've quite enjoyed this eccentric town, witches feuding with humans. Humans hunting witches. I have to say, I've never seen a coexistence laced with such hate and animosity. It's rather appealing. So, I'm sure you can understand why we stepped in and offered Elijah what he so desperately wanted," Darick says, casually walking near a post. The synergy around the circle fluctuates as he passes through like a chartered soul entering another dimension. It wavers again as he steps back out.

"What did you do to Elijah?" Evan questions.

"Same thing he did to Catherine. Fed him to the demon," Darick states with a crooked smile.

"You reap what you sow. But I think though, Elijah said it best. *"It was the divine will of Hecate"*," Louis adds and rises from his chair. "I don't know about the divine will, but Evan, I still think you should re-establish your rank in the Brotherhood. You made it look *so easy* killing the innocent." Louis grips the back of the chair and stares at Evan. "Come on, what do you say, Ev? It would be like old times."

"I've made my choice, Louis. Never again will I put myself in servitude for the Brotherhood," Evan coldly replies. The sound of feet shuffling grips my immediate attention. Evan and I turn and watch as Silas brings Hannah up through the hatchway. Her hands are tied with an old, twisted rope behind her back. Visible rips and tears run along her filthy dress exposing bloodstained flesh. Strips of hair hang over her clammy face as Silas shoves her toward Darick. He catches her and clamps his hands around her frail shoulders.

She whimpers as he forces her to look up. "Here's the girl," Darick taunts with a sly, devious grin.

"Get your fucking hands off her!" I growl and start to lunge forward. Evan blocks me, throwing his arm across my chest and pushes me back.

Louis shifts obstructing my sight, we're nose to nose as he growls back, "Where's the book?"

Evan slips the book out from inside his jacket. "Here, take it," he says and then glares over to Darick. "Now…let her go."

Louis backs off and flips through the timeworn pages. But with each page, his facial expression becomes tauter and more bitter. "This isn't the book. What do you think we are, Evan? Gullible? You've glamoured the book, thinking we wouldn't notice?" He hurls the book across the room and makes a tsking noise chiding Evan for his feeble attempt. "It's a good thing, Silas here is not as dumb as he looks because he made himself a copy of the basic ritual." He glances toward Silas.

Silas fumbles with a slip of paper in his hands, shaking and trembling as if the scribbly words will combust into flames any second now. "*Y-yeah*, yeah, I have it," he stutters out.

Louis walks away and grumbles, "I should've seen it coming, Darick. Cunning bastard. Well…" he pauses and looks over his shoulder. "then I bet you won't see this coming."

Darick grips Hannah by the head and jerks in one swift movement. Bones crack as he snaps her neck and then he releases her. Her tousled blonde hair still covers her face, but I catch the last glimpse of fright riddling inside her vague, dull eyes. She falls to the floor motionless and I unleash everything I have. Red-hot flames unite with my fury.

"*Nooo!*" Silas shouts and charges toward Darick. "*Why!* Why did you do that to her?!" He punches and swings like a madman, but Darick kicks him so hard he's like a whirlwind zooming through the air. An uproar of wind and fire prevails over Silas' wails and outcries as havoc begins. He scurries toward the circle and bumps the candles over. Several roll and spin out of his way as if he's on his own rampage.

Darick shifts and slams into Evan and they crash into a nearby wall. Darick's fiery arm presses against Evan while his other hand holds a sharp tipped dagger at Evan's throat. I shift directly behind Louis before he manages another gust of wind and squeeze my arm tightly around his neck. Some may think they're immortal but once I rip his beating heart out of his fucking chest— he's no different than the rest. He grunts and claws at my face. Desperation eats through his veins as he tries to breathe out. I catch his wheezing words. "*Fuck you,*" he lips and channels a sudden burst of air downward. It sends us backward, but my levitational force keeps me from landing on my ass. My flames melt through his overcoat. Smoke and fire rise consuming the air as he struggles against me. The soles of his shoes scrape against the flooring trying to find some leverage. He knows it's only a matter of time as his elemental magick starts to dwindle away. Despair can do a lot of things to a man, but recklessness can be the final blow. Louis lets go of my arm and ushers out the last ounce of power he has. A whirling mass of air coils around and as it slithers toward us I lessen my grip. His mouth gapes open, sucking in a breath and I use the turbulent wind to my advantage and engulf it in fire. I condense the churning inferno and thrust it into his mouth. Burning him up from the inside out.

Embers and ash ascend like doomsday, and I feel like punishing and destroying anything in my path. My vision turns red. Streams of burning vapor waver from yellow, orange, and crimson. Not only are my hands encased with fire, but my entire body is a torrent of flames. I march a path toward Darick, scorching the wooden floor with each step taken.

"Back off!" Darick seethes. Evan circles him, a trace of blood drips down his neck. Darick effortlessly tosses the flaming dagger between his hands preparing for his next move. Evan crouches and nods as I strike out orbs of fire. Distracting Darick, Evan shifts in and starts pounding him with his fists like a hurricane. Each hit stifles Darick's element until he's down on one knee. Bloody and battered he mouths, "You may have taken me down, but Namtar will rise." Evan summons a gush of water and throws Darick back, but he keeps his momentum and quickly snatches the blade.

I stoop down and glare over Darick's face. "I will hunt down every single one of you and annihilate your kind."

Evan takes Darick's weapon and stabs him straight in the heart. A flutter of fire rises and converts into a billow of putrid smoke. I glance over to Evan as

Darick takes his last breath. "Where's Silas?" I ask. While we were taking out the Brotherhood, Silas' whereabouts were lost in the fray. Anger, fury, and blinding rage fuel my need to decimate, but as Evan and I turn around, a new emotion surfaces. Alarm.

Silas sits in the midst of an unprotected circle. A few candles burn a partial glow, but others are chasing and igniting the sagging sheets that cover the windows. Fire blazes along the westward wall like a roaring furnace. The temperature rises as Silas chants a string of foreign words. "He's invoking the demon," Evan says.

"Silas…what are you doing?" I demand and carefully maneuver toward him.

He jerks his head up, his morbid eyes stream with inklike tears that roll down his cheeks. "Surrendering myself to Namtar."

"You don't have to do this," Evan says inching up beside me.

Silas drops his head downward, his hair saturated with sweat, and then his body twitches. His mouth hangs open as if he's gagging on something, and then he pukes all over the crumpled paper before him. His shoulders shake as he laughs. He wipes his mouth off with the back of his hand and replies in a grisly tone, "*It's already been done.*"

Chapter Thirty

"*Silas*, listen to me…" I express limiting the fire around me. As Evan steps forward, he's blocked by a field of energy. It hovers and glistens like a web stretching from post to post.

Silas gives a twisted grin and replies, "This is your fault, David. Hannah would have been mine if you hadn't showed up here." He's hunched over, still on his hands and knees like a wounded animal. Shivering as if the burning flames are a cold winter's breeze. His eyes are nothing but shadowy black pits. I know we're too late.

A howl breaks through the crackling fire, but it morphs into a blood-curdling scream from Silas as his body splits open. A beast rises from his corpse like its shedding off dead skin.

Namtar stands much like the image depicted from the grimoire. Half man, half beast with horns jutting from his jawbone that curve toward the ground. Black hair as slick as glass and eyes that gleam with your own reflection. He shakes off the remains like he's disgusted and rolls back his massive shoulders. The sheer height of him is enough to make a mortal swallow in terror and run the other way. Evan silently motions to me and I coast my eyes over to the sketchy circle. The candles Silas knocked over leaves an opening and the perfect exit for Namtar. But as I'm about to shift Namtar speaks. The language is jarring and unknown, but then he rumbles out, "Sweet taste of the willing but more compelling is the unwilled." His skin drips with blood as smoke flares from his nostrils, and I know time is slipping away. I have to seal the pentagram.

"The book…*my book*…where is it?" Namtar snarls.

"Why would you need it now?" Evan questions trying to divert the demon's attention. "You've already made the progression. What's the point in having the book now?"

"The point?" Namtar growls and scrapes his horns along the hardwood floor. "If you don't know the magnitude it holds for me, then get out of my sight!" In one wave of his clawed hand, he sails Evan across the area. And then he snaps his head in my direction. "Fools may worm their way into my realm, but they don't behold the precious things they will lose."

I grimace unsure of his words, but as he crouches forward I see the intent in his demonic eyes. Eradicate, and that's exactly what he wants to do to me. My hands move upward ready to force an outburst of flames, but as my fire flows through my hands and surround my fingertips something happens. The element, the energy instantly pulls out of me like a giant magnetic tug. Rooting out and weakening my powers. I jump away from the circle and yell, "Evan?!"

Evan grips his shoulder like he's hurt and stands. "He's fully evolved now, and he can extract our magick *and* our elements," he says and rushes toward Hannah's body. "Get her. Hurry! We have to get out of here." He starts chanting a mixture of phrases while I grab the body.

Namtar throws his head back and sadistically laughs. The smoldering air clings to my lungs, the flames have increased and a foul scent of death wafts throughout. A post on the far side gives way, cracking and splitting apart. The building is defined in an eerie afterglow formed from Namtar, lingering throughout the fiery blaze. Smoke becomes more of a problem preventing any clear view of where he is. Then the sound of heavy footsteps lurch to another post and it collapses. "Any magick we use, he'll absorb. Come on, the spell I cast won't last long!" Evan yells and shields us as charred boards and joists fall. I can barely see the hatch leading below and barrel through the sea of fire. Lunging over burning debris, I skid to the opening and swiftly drop down. Evan's right behind me. "Which way?" he asks.

I cough out smoke and mentally search for our bond. Hannah's essence beats with life within and I know which direction to go. "This way!"

We retrace our path veering from one dusky tunnel to the next until the bond is so strong it hammers through my body. "David? Why are we carrying this

corpse with us if you know Hannah's down here?"
Evan asks careening around a corner.

"If I left the body up there and the demon
decided to eat it, burn it, who knows what, then Hannah
wouldn't be able to switch. I'm not a hundred percent
sure how this spirit thing works and I'm not taking any
chances."

We journey to the second narrow channel and
find Elroy kneeling in front of a blocked corridor, his
hands grasping the hexed stone laced with eccentric
magical links. "I almost have it," he grunts as he
reverses the spell. He glides two fingers upward like
he's plucking a tight tethered strap and then a loud
plinking noise reverberates. The translucent veil
shrivels up and funnels into a bundle of willow sticks in
his other hand. He rises steadying himself along one of
the rocks nearby. "The boulder was just an illusion.
One of Elijah's added protections for his spell work.
You can go in now," he says gruffly.

I snap my fingers and shed a glimmer of light in
the dank, moldy chamber. Bodies spread across the
floor like an undertaker's lair— mangled and marred
with a rotting stench saturating the air. Some are
chained to the walls and some bound to the ground. But
none twitch with a breath of life. I feel her before I see
her, tucked in the farthest corner. Her knees are bent
close to her chest, her head sags against the cold stone
as if she's in a state of sleep. I sidestep around the dead
and gently ease the body in my arms down beside her.
"Hannah…it's time. Come on, babe," I urge and scoot
back. I've never seen someone spirit walk before, but if

it's true what they say, then I know our bond kept me from keeling over the moment I saw Darick break her neck. The body must have been recently deceased when Hannah utilized her spirit ability. Evan and Elroy stand in the shadows as a fine white mist suspends over the body. And then a ghostly image of Hannah floats upward like an ethereal shape over to her true self. The moment she opens her blue grey eyes she springs from her huddled position and dives into my arms. *"Oh! David…"* she whispers and tightens her hold on me.

"You did good, Hannah. The Brotherhood never suspected anything," I praise her and gently kiss the side of her cheek. A warmth of comfort wraps around me knowing she's safe and in my arms.

Elroy sidles up beside us. "I told you, Hannah, that one day you might see what you got is a gift," he says and taps his temple. "Smarts and a little witchery can save your hide sometimes."

Hannah tries to offer him a small smile, but worry etches in her tone, "What about my sisters and Grandmother Greta?"

"They're safe. They're with Gemma," Evan states and then drops his look downward in remorse. "I'm sorry about your mother and your father, Hannah." Fragments of her parents' clothing are piled up in the center like a symbolic token of the slain. "The demon is above burning down the building. So we don't have much time." As soon as Evan turns toward the passageway, a ball of fire shoots through the shaft. A grating, diabolical chuckle follows as the stones shake, and dirt puffs out from the crevices in the wall.

I swing Hannah behind me and force out a little bit of my fire, crafting a shield of sorts around us. My energy is drained but if we can make it back to the house we may have a fighting chance. Elroy hobbles next to Evan and spouts, "You got enough power in ya to bring up the rear and keep'em from burnin' our breeches off?" He squints one eye at Evan waiting for his reply. Evan nods. "Good, then I'll lead us." Elroy guides us through the trembling path. An intensive wave of heat and light ripples by and burrows inside the cracks and seams. Elroy moves with a faster pace but adds caution as he scours the underground arteries. Each path becomes stuffier and ill-lit. And then Namtar speaks in his fiendish tongue whispering through the walls as if he's part of the underlying structure.

Another blaze travels over our heads, and as we duck, I spot the trapdoor and a small speck of light filtering in. Elroy waves a hand and a rope promptly lowers like it's obeying a simple command and a stepladder unfolds. I lift Hannah up first and glance over my shoulder making sure Evan's still with us and climb through the opened hatch.

"There's nothing left of our home, nothing to ward off the demon…" Hannah says lowering herself to the broken clay pots and damaged plants on the floor. She picks up a few stems and scattered pieces of a white snakeroot and shakes her head. "There has to be something?"

"Whatever we conjure will only magnify Namtar, but for how long he can maintain it, I don't know," Evan remarks and tries to open the main door.

He jiggles the old iron knob, but it doesn't budge. He walks over to a window, releases the metal latch, and finds it's sealed. "These are not jammed by accident," he says studying the filmy glow hemmed inside the frame.

"Do you think the demon performed one of my father's spell crafts to lock us in?" Hannah asks.

"Possibly. I'm pretty sure Namtar's using whatever means necessary to keep us here. Every soul he's taken he'll gain their knowledge or power—" Evan explains.

Elroy quickly adds, "Elijah had once said to me that it was goin' to take quite a bit from him to see his work come into fruition, and then every man, woman, and child would bow before him." He coldly chuckles. "Well I don't see anyone bowing, do you? Damn convoluted fool."

Hannah nudges me. "My mother may have a counterspell somewhere in the kitchen," she says with a touch of hope in her voice. Before I have a chance to reapproach the idea she's halfway there. Handcrafted shelves line the back-kitchen wall, rustic pots and pans hang from oak carved pegs. As Hannah slips a warped blue pan off, a hidden compartment slowly rolls out. Various dark colored bottles for tinctures and tonics display like they're in a witchcraft museum. A stash of dried herbs and medicinal plants, carefully secured by a coarse piece of twine, falls to the floor. She fumbles through her mother's secret supply and nervously bites her lip as she pulls out a cloth covered jar. "Maybe we can use this to find another way out?" she questions untying the burlap.

"What is it?" I ask taking the jar and look it over.

"It's a jar of spines, that's what she called them, but they're really a limacodid. A slug moth. Each spine is venomous, but I used them to find the weak links in some of my father's spells. If there's any fragility in them, then we'll find it."

I nod my head like I'm on board and start to turn, but then an eruption of fire catches me off guard. Fire bores through the exhaust vent above the stove and whips out a long, forklike tongue as if it's a serpent getting a whiff of foraging prey.

Hannah yells, "David!" as it lashes across my back. I cinch my hand around Hannah's and run toward the living room area.

"That fire thieving demon is inside the house somewhere!" I shout over to Evan. Severed pieces of furniture and wooden fixtures jolt upward as if they're bewitched. They hover and spin madly around and then fly by us, some barely meet the walls before they burst into flames.

"He's using Silas' element," Evan says blocking a wooden candle holder as it soars past him. The shards clump together making a bigger fire, stacking, and melting into the walls, and confining the space. A low cynical chuckling thunders through the house. Overhead, bleak clouds of smoke quickly outrival the long-standing supports and the ceiling is immersed. Elroy hacks and coughs. "The son of a bitch is goin' to suffocate us to death," he hollers out stumbling toward Evan.

I feel like we are trapped inside a giant tree while it burns us up like a thousand-degree oven. My own element can scarcely keep Hannah safe. The flames whip out hungry for a taste of flesh. It's become so thick and dark with fumes I can't see Evan or even Elroy, but when one of them says something, I move closer.

"David?!" Evan shouts over the roaring fire.

"Yeah…we're over here," I yell back, keeping Hannah by my side. A flurry of red shimmers a few feet away as a crossbeam falls. "David, we have to get out of here. The house is going to burn to the ground and take us with it," Hannah urges. I peer around looking at the fucking rat trap the demon has us in. A widespread blaze raids through her family's home like it's a box of matchsticks. And if any of us wield our power to fight against it—it drains us, and it's used against us. *Fuck!* I'm beyond pissed, but the one thing that scares me the most is if something happens to Hannah. I cannot let her die in this monstrosity Namtar has created. I have to find a way out of here or die trying.

I shield her body with my own and trudge over the enflamed scattered debris. And as we reach Evan beside the doorway an ear-deafening boom ricochets out. The floor shakes, the windows rattle and even the fiery walls tremble.

"What was that?" Hannah asks peeking through the smoke.

"I…I don't know," I reply waiting for the demon to jump down from the rafters and attack.

Evan raises his scorched hand out. "Something's outside…"

"Is it the demon?" Elroy voices through the blackened air.

Ice interlaces with the binding energy around the doorjamb and spreads like a cruel winter storm. The flaming tendrils squirm and shrink away and then a pounding violently strikes the wood-grained door. Splinters of cedar and ice explode through the entrance and in steps Marc. He's unscathed by the demonry but he doesn't waste any time as he calls out, "David?"

"It's okay. He's a friend." I mouth next to Hannah's ear and lead her out. As I pass Marc I quickly nod, there's a shit-ton of things I want to say, but now is not the time for expressions of gratitude. I just want to get Hannah as far away from here as possible. Evan and Elroy shadow our path until we see Mr. Worthington. He's standing just on the fringes of the property, both hands spread out like he's holding onto a magical veil. Streams of white and gold energy move like a continuous flowing spectrum and constrain the fire.

He glances over to me in his hooded cloak and says, "First car, get in. This circle won't hold forever." He closes his hands briefly and the veil sways as Marc shifts through it. Hannah and I jump in the backseat as Evan and Elroy take the front. Marc slides in on the other side and shuts the door. Daniel lifts his hands up once more and asserts a spell I'd never heard before. As if the tips of his fingers were fused to the veil he flickers one at a time, a gold strand shackles to the earth, and then a white light courses through like it's interlocking his words. Binding and concealing Namtar in a provisional imprisonment. A black car behind us starts up and blends in with the twilight. I turn back and wonder why they're heading toward the town.

"They're going to make sure there are no traces of you and Evan there," Marc replies. His breath still huffs out an iciness as if we're standing in the middle of Antarctica.

I swallow and taste the charred smoke lingering in my lungs and start to say, "Thanks…"

But he quickly replies, "Don't thank me yet, David. We're not out of the woods." He lowers his head peering out of the tinted windows like he's still on the alert. Daniel takes the driver's seat and glances back at everyone. "Is everyone okay?" he questions sternly looking at each one of us. He turns back around and slips a few healing vials out from his dark cloak. "Here take this, it will help restore your energy. Time and rest are what you need to truly heal but this will suffice for now."

"David looks like he's been charbroiled. I don't think I've ever seen him look this bad before," Marc comments.

"Yeah, well I don't think you'd look any better if you walked through the gates of hell like I just did," I remark shaking my head.

"I take it you're done playing with fire now?" Marc leans over and narrows his brown eyes at me.

"Fuck no, fire is my element. It's part of me. Just because some jacked-up demon steals it and mimics it, doesn't mean I'd turn my back against it." I let out a sigh full of smoke and add, "I just never thought I'd be roasted to death inside a house, that's all."

"You know, that's how we figured out where you two were…follow the flames and sure enough you'll find David," Marc states and then faces Hannah. "I'm sorry I didn't introduce myself earlier. I'm Marcus Del Dante, but everyone just calls me Marc."

Hannah takes his hand and as they shake, Mr. Worthington drives us away from the quaint little town of Mistcove. Evan rests his head against the back of the seat and asks, "You have the book?"

Daniel doesn't veer his eyes away from the road but replies, "I do. Mailing it as soon as you received it was smart, Evan. But contacting one of our witch informants, Mr. Whitman the postmaster, and having it appear on my doorstep that night was impeccable. Acquiring something that's a threat to our rede is a must, and I'm afraid to say this, but it will have to be taken to the council of witches. The Seven."

I scoot closer to the front. "Wait, I thought they weren't banded together?" I ask as the backwoods feel more unreal. The towering trees and the Lover's Leap cliffside drift off into the distance. The haze of smoke highlighting the Wolfenstein's home fades in with the lake's fog.

Worthington ushers his words over his shoulder, "They were not, but since the Brotherhood has unearthed demons like the one Evan had told me about, Namtar, then their reasons to assemble a council became mutual."

Hannah wiggles forward. "What about the rest of my family? We can't just leave them?"

Mr. Worthington sends a glance toward Evan. "Do you have an idea where they are?"

"Yes, cross this next road and six miles east, but their aunt has the area concealed," Evan answers and offers Elroy some of his vial. Elroy pushes it away and flops his head against the window. He's the one that looks the worst. Between the Brotherhood and the inferno, I can only imagine how he's feeling right now. He's not a young witch filled with vigor and embodied with a threshold to protect a lifemate. It's not in him anymore. But his love for the girls keeps him grounded. As Evan gently eases him back against the seat, a firetruck cruises up with lights and sirens wailing. Daniel swiftly moves the car to the shoulder of the road. With the calmness of a flame dancing over a candle, he parks the car and strides toward the firetruck as if he's the one that called the fire in. He flags it down and they immediately stop, not because he's dressed in some cloak and dagger look, but as a human reaching out for help. If you blinked you wouldn't have noticed the change he underwent, and the control he easily constructed to hail down a firetruck in pursuit. At first, the words are incoherent that toss between the driver and Daniel.

But then I hear him say, "I'm sorry to have bothered you. There was a bonfire and I thought it was getting out of control out by the lake…" Daniel says with a convincing tone, but quickly after he speaks, their eyes glaze over and they nod like they're in some kind of trance. Voices linger in and out and Daniel abruptly turns and heads for the car. And the firetruck that was in hot pursuit for Hannah's home quickly makes a U-turn and drives off. Mr. Worthington settles back into his seat, throws the shifter into drive, and looks at Hannah in the rearview mirror and says, "We're going to take your family to a safe place. Have you ever been to Wyoming?"

The End

Epilogue

Moorcroft, Wyoming is where the Arcane University is located and hidden from the human world. It's one of the few factions that carry all the elements and instill the magick that's in all of us. After a few days, Mr. Worthington has everything in order and we finally pull into a private driveway. A row of lush pine trees outline the private road and up to a three-story log house. It reminds me of a ski villa in Aspen, Colorado. I recognize the house immediately as it sits nestled within the forest. It was previously Marc and Alyssa's home. The front of the house has large glass windows showcasing the massive, vaulted ceiling inside. All the lights are on, which makes it look illuminated like the Taj Mahal. A deck wraps completely around the second floor and a small stone path leads from the front door to the driveway. The home is concealed and secured by white candles that encircle the area, each marks an essential part of a protection spell.

A true untainted magick hangs in the air and the unquestionable sense of being around familiar witches draws near. Alyssa is the first one I spot coming out of the house. "David!" she exclaims rushing over and hugs me. Her bright blue eyes drift over to Hannah. "Hi, I'm Alyssa. I'm so glad you guys made it safely," she says fervently gripping Hannah's hand like she's one of the family. She quickly introduces herself to Elroy and then darts a look toward her father. "Someone from the council is here and they want to speak with you. If you want, Marc and I can take the book to the Arcane and have it guarded there like we did the other demon book?"

Daniel takes in a pensive breath before he answers, "It needs to be guarded, but we need the council to help decrypt it and assimilate a plan to destroy the demon." He glances at Hannah and adds, "The rest of your family will be here soon, and once we can gather enough information about Namtar we will go before the council of seven."

Hannah steals a moment and looks at Marc, Alyssa, Daniel, the house, and then the woods. It's a lot for her to take in. Everything has changed for her, and I can sense she's trying to absorb it all at once. "What about the Nakoa and the people in Mistcove? Someone will remember what's happened?"

Daniel softens his demeanor and replies, "No one will remember. Our mind sweep spell will resolve that issue. The only thing anyone will know is there was a fire, and it took a family. Your name, *Wolfenstein*, will be like a vague ghostly imprint in Mistcove so that we can keep you safe. The elders there will continue on in silence and try to restore some balance because your father had embedded black magick within the very soil of that town. Try to think of it as a new beginning for everyone. All witches go through transitions, some wander into the dark and some seek the light. As I'm sure you saw with Elijah and how your mother was lost to his endless greed. But I want *you* to know a new world has opened up for you, Hannah. It will be up to you, though, in deciding how your journey will unfold."

Earth Bound *coming in 2021*

Karli Rush

Other books by karli Rush

Crescent Bound
Raven Bound
Demon Bound
Shadow Bound
Ice Bound

Daylight
Midnight

The House
Withering Bones

Nine Lives

Memoirs of a Superhero

Let Your Heart Drive

Seducing a Mermaid

Pine Needles

If you would like to keep up with the author's work, or any new stories coming soon, then follow her on —
Facebook
Goodreads
Instagram
Blog